Anita Mooring
braiding fiction and technology

Decoy U: the case of the
Conniving Contractors
By: Anita Mooring

Using cutting-edge technology, Grit Inc. employs hundreds of cell phones users for surveillance.

The software program Leo Grit created tracks the location of each phone and enables Leo to alert the user that a target is in their vicinity. No one notices the college students talking on their phones, secretly recording and uploading information to the server.

When Leo decides to take his company to the next level and bids on a multimillion-dollar government contract, he's unprepared for the competition's ruthless attacks to damage his company's credibility.

Will Leo allow the large and powerful companies to bully him into submission?

Or will he use his hacking skills to retaliate in a way they won't soon forget?

Exciting and fast paced, *Decoy U* will have you furiously turning pages while Grit's fight for survival becomes far more personal than Leo could have ever imagined.

Decoy U – Eyes & Ears Everywhere –Case of the Conniving Contractors
Mooring, Anita
Copyright 2015 by Anita Mooring
ISBN: 978-1-937334-68-0
First Edition Electronic February 2016

Chapter 1

"Colored lights flash across the crowded room as Denise and Stacy push their way toward the back of the club. Smoke curled and rose toward the dark ceiling, paying homage to the decadent aura. Dressed seductively, women and men hunt desperately for someone to take home tonight," Leo Grit spoke in a low, mocking tone to the decoys through his microphone as he watched them ease their way to participate in a different type of hunt.

A tall, dark bald guy, who could win a Mr. T lookalike contest without trying, stood with legs braced apart in front of a red cord leading to a staircase. Unlike the two outside at the entrance, this one didn't pay the girls any special attention. It'd take more than a sexy body to get past him.

"Time to work." Leo's voice normalized, all hint of joking disappeared. He couldn't see the dance floor, wall to wall people danced to some funky beat.

"Stacy, move closer to the security guy so I can get a good look at his face," Leo instructed. Denise continued onto the bar and took a seat. Stacy, a cute blonde with bluish-gray eyes, nice athletic, body and long legs, stopped a few feet from the security guard and dug into her large purse. Leo maneuvered the lens in the small camera embedded in her necklace to take a picture of the giant.

"Got it. Get in position, Tag should be coming through the roped area soon. He'll pass the beer bottle to you or Denise. Slip it in your purse and head for the bathroom to upload the prints. I'm ready," Leo said, watching red, green, and blue dots move on the large monitor in front of him.

Fortunately for the company and this assignment Tag's cousin managed the club, allowing him to move freely without security challenges. Although the waitress in the VIP section signed on as a decoy Leo couldn't use her, personnel and some patrons were scanned for cameras and other electronics. Strict security measures included covering camera lenses on cell with colored tape in that area which made this job more difficult and possibly dangerous.

Leo equipped Tag with a small camera embedded in his eyeglasses which didn't include audio or video, but the client assured him the still photos Tag uploaded earlier was sufficient to make a preliminary identification.

Shelly's red dot flashed on the monitor, informing him she got his instructions. Denise's followed. Adrenaline pumping, Leo rubbed his hands together. Regardless of how much they prepped for a job anything could go wrong in the field and he needed to be ready to respond quickly.

His gaze fastened on the screen as Denise's camera came online, providing another angle of Satan's Den, the popular nightclub near Charlotte. Loud music, dim lighting, and the large crowd added various levels of difficulty to the job of locating and positively identifying Rolando Phelps—a person of interest for his client. Tag's red dot headed toward the girls.

"Tag's on the move, be ready. Easy … easy." His brow furrowed as he leaned forward, staring at Tag's dot moving toward the bar and settling next to Denise.

"Hey, sexy lady," Tag said, his angular face appearing on the side screen next to the large monitor. He ran his fingers through reddish-blond hair, pulling it back from his forehead. Dark brown eyes glanced at the necklace on Denise's neck and then back at her.

Denise, three or four inches shorter than Tag's six feet, pushed his chest and waved her hand in front of her face. "*Phew*, you've been drinking."

Tag laughed and leaned into her. His fingertips brushed against her dark shoulder-length hair for a second and then tapped her chin. Stacy stood and headed to the bathroom to secure a stall and prepare to scan the prints on the bottle.

Denise glanced in her direction.

"Good girl," Leo murmured, his gaze fastened on the action. "Time to move, but not too fast in case someone's watching."

"Not too much that I can't buy a pretty girl a drink," Tag said, waving his hand at her partially-full glass. "Give me a beer and give the pretty lady whatever she wants," he told the bartender.

Denise's long, brown fingers covered the top of her glass and then pushed him away. "No thank you." She hefted her large purse on her shoulder and muscled her way through the crowd to the bathroom. Once inside she coughed. Stacy stepped out a stall and handed her a felt bag. Denise walked inside the stall.

"Using your fingertips, place the glass in the container," Leo instructed, watching closely. "Now push that green button on the bottom."

Denise pushed it. Nothing happened.

"Fuck! Hold on." Leo rebooted the remote device. "Piece of shit," he murmured while waiting for it to return online. A minute later the green light on his console flashed. "Try again."

She pressed the button. The light in front of him flashed for a few seconds as it transmitted fingerprints from the bottle to his computer. When the transfer completed, he exhaled, pleased they'd completed the most difficult part of the assignment.

"Go back into the club, dance, mingle, I'll get back with you in a minute."

Denise stuck the device with the bottle into her oversized purse then went to the mirror and applied lipstick. Curvier than Stacy, she tugged on the hem of her dress, washed her hands, and left the room as two females walked in.

Aware of his client's short time-line, Leo signed into the FBI's NGI (Next Generation Identification) system to find a match. It didn't take long to get a hit and confirm Phelps identity. He clapped his hands with a sense of satisfaction and then sent the client still photos of Phelps with his friends in the VIP section earlier, the beer bottle, and the results from NGI. He glanced at the financial clock embedded in the system as it charged the client for every minute they were on the job.

"Oh yeah," he yelled at the high dollar amount remaining to complete this assignment. Noise from the club drew his attention. Leaning back in his chair, he pushed up his glasses and watched various faces flow across the monitor.

An email alert registered on the screen. Leo read the message from his client.

Get your people out of there – ten minutes.

"Time to go, my beauties. You're on the clock for an additional thirty minutes, plus your one hour travel time. Just another added bonus from the top information company in the whole US of A." He chuckled. "Great job guys, drive safely," he told Denise, Stacy, and Tag. "Drop off the equipment tomorrow afternoon and email your reports."

Three red lights flashed as the girls pushed their way to the exit, avoiding grasping hands and overzealous guys. Once they cleared the parking lot, and were on the highway, five minutes had passed.

"I'm out," Tag said.

"Good job, you made this work by accessing the VIP area."

"Does that mean I get a little extra? I have labs next week."

Leo chuckled. Dealing primarily with college students he'd heard all kinds of requests for extra pay. Tonight Tag earned it. "That's exactly what that means. Drive careful." He keyed in everyone's pay for this job and sent the information to Cherise, his office manager. At the end of the week she'd release funds into their bank accounts and send emails detailing their earnings.

Still hyped, he replayed the live feed of the club. People jumped up and down, twisting, turning, arms raised, heads thrown back, faces alit with pleasure to a beat he felt through the distance. Had he ever been that carefree? Happy?

How long had it been since he'd gone dancing or on a date? *Too long.* Leo ran his fingers through his shaggy brown hair and watched a few moments longer. Seems he'd been doing a lot of living from the sidelines lately. Not that he had much to complain about, starting a company that evolved into a decoy/spy/intelligence business hadn't been his original goal, he'd simply wanted to redeem himself. Offer something positive to the community after the damage he'd done with Venom, a lethal virus he created in college. Some days he still wasn't sure how he stumbled into the decoy part of it, and why it was so hard to believe his crazy idea to put all of this together worked.

His gaze zeroed in on a pretty brunette, her hair flew around her with cape-like abilities. Make-up didn't completely conceal the scar on her chin. It stood out on the monitor in contrast to her otherwise perfect features. She turned abruptly when someone nearby lifted their cell phone taking pictures. Everyone had something to hide.

Privacy became a thing of the past as long as cell phones capable of on-the-spot recording were in the hands of the public. Thousands of people recorded everything they saw on the streets and uploaded it to the Internet which fueled his idea for a business. Pay people to use their cell phones and upload picture or videos to his program. Students always looked for ways to make money and signed up as E&Es: eyes and ears.

Just as the brunette turned from the camera, Leo turned from that niggle of doubt in the back of his mind that said no matter how many college students and clients he helped, he was nowhere near repaying his debt. If the authorities ever discovered he'd been behind the destruction of the finance company several years ago he'd see the inside of prison.

Tired of the loud music and reminders of past mistakes, he sent the client their final report and prepared to go home. At the mention of live footage, the client asked to see it. A few moments later he sent the file and logged off.

Leo looked at the clock, stretched, and yawned. Today had been long and profitable. At this rate he'd add another server to the four others in the back and hire another technician to work with Craig on equipment the decoys used. Tonight proved once again he needed someone more skilled to prevent malfunctions at critical moments.

The silence in the building suited his mood. It'd been a lengthy week. Tomorrow he'd sleep late, come in around noon, and catch up on a few things. Two jobs sat in the queue for tomorrow afternoon and evening. Barb, his training instructor, would accompany the decoys, and Craig would work the board as Leo had done tonight.

He grabbed his bike from his office, locked up, and headed to the home his grandparents left him not far from work or the university. In his junior year he moved into the four bedrooms, three and a half bath, ranch-style brick house, thinking it'd help him get more female action.

That never happened.

Zeke and Nathan, an IT major from Honduras, shared the place with him and had fewer dates than him. A year into his graduate work they moved out. He turned a bedroom into a computer lab where he fed his creative demon with variations of Ghost and Venom, his two crowning achievements.

Outside, the fading scent of jasmine, motor oil, and exhaust fumes teased his senses as he pedaled out the parking lot on to the road. Moonlight filtered through the trees, offering patches of light on the asphalt along with widely spaced apart street posts. Cool night air brushed against his face as he traveled the few blocks home.

Thunder rumbled in the distance. Clouds hid the moon. Leo picked up the pace. His house sat at the end of the long street. He turned into the driveway, circled around his parked truck to the back patio. Outdoor lights flicked on as he approached. Large drops of cold rain hit his back as he pushed open the door and pulled his bike inside.

After disengaging his security system, he reengaged it for the night. An old Daft Punk song streamed through speakers from his digital music collection, which played all day. Thirsty, he grabbed a cola from the refrigerator and leaned against the counter. Remnants of coffee, ginger, and baked fish—a combination of his breakfast and lunch— lingered in the kitchen. He yawned and stretched. As the adrenaline ebbed, tiredness settled on his shoulder.

He kicked off his shoes and headed to the bedroom to clean up, maybe watch a little TV before bed. Showered and dressed in jogging pants, he half listened to the news while trimming his beard. At some point the screen blurred, the newscaster's face elongated making his eyes look ridiculously big. "Now for the latest in a series of financial suicides. Kern McDermot, Jenny Howard, Patrick Ling, Curst Ioni, Paige Manning are the latest victims who took their lives because of a financial melt-down today." He pointed his finger. "You've been a bad boy, Leo the police are going to find you very soon."

Leo sat up, chest heaving and gasping for air. He pushed the covers off and held his forehead in the palm of his hand. The TV continued to play and he searched for the remote just as the news reporter said.

"… in the parking lot of a local club in Charlotte … Three fatalities in what police believe was a gang-related shooting in the parking lot. The names of the victims haven't been released."

Chapter 2

The ground smoldered. Noon temperatures soared to the high nineties. Heat rose like a serpent from the asphalt and curled around Leo's sweat dampened shirt searching for his skin. He blinked to clear the disorienting haze from his vision. Hot and dripping with sweat, Leo stopped his bike in the parking lot of the office building he owned in the middle of a small, suburban neighborhood.

The beige two-story structure housed several small startups on the first floor. Grit Inc., his company, operated from the entire second floor. The purchase took a huge portion of his savings, but he needed the space to install extra security for his computer hardware: Ghost. Once all the offices on the first floor were occupied, the financial burden would lighten—at least that's what he told himself every time he saw the 'For Lease' sign on the three remaining offices.

A young boy dressed in cut-off shorts and a yellow tank top pulled a wagon loaded with small boxes across the parking lot. Leo looked at the kid's worn rubber-soled sneakers and winced at how thin they appeared. Ignoring the sun baking his neck, he fiddled with his keys while watching the boy approach.

"Buy a box of microwave popcorn or chocolate chip cookies to help our little league team, mister?"

Leo looked down at the kid and the load in his wagon. The boy couldn't have been more than nine or ten. Any chocolate in those boxes would be goo beneath this heat. "You play football?"

"Yes, sir." He stared up at Leo, waiting.

"You any good?" Leo reached in his pocket and fingered a bill he'd placed there earlier.

"Yes, sir, I run the ball." His chest rose slightly as a toothy grin blossomed on his face.

Leo pulled out a twenty and handed it to the kid. "How much will this buy me?"

The kid's eyes widened as his gaze latched onto the bill, swallowing hard. "A lot, sir."

Minutes later Leo strolled through the office whistling as the chilly air cooled his burnt skin. He rolled his bike down the hall and carried a bag on his arm loaded with popcorn and cookies. Voices from the back reached him as he turned to secure his wheels in the side closet. He peeped around the corner to see Stacy and Denise talking with Barb.

Stacy waved. "Hey, did you hear what happened at that club, Satan's Den, last night?"

He poured a cup of coffee. "Like what?" Inhaling the aroma, and appreciating the steam curling toward him, he blew on it.

"There was a shooting in the parking lot." Her eyes lit as she repeated what she'd heard on the news. "Some gangs were fighting and three people were killed. Good thing we left when we did. It happened not long after."

He took a careful sip of his drink as thoughts of last night's job rolled through his mind. That was his third job for that client. Leo wasn't exactly sure which government agency Mr. Thompson, the client, represented. The man never answered Leo's questions regarding his department or how he found his company, Grit Inc.

"Have they released anything about the shooting or is this just another gang war?" he asked, curious if Rolando Phelps had been involved.

"No, not yet," she said, turned, and walked toward the training room with Denise, leaving him to wonder if his company had been used to setup Phelps. Coincidences made him nervous, he'd recheck his security to make sure his system couldn't be compromised.

Barb waved at him. "Can I talk to you for a minute?"

He looked down at her, nodded, and headed to his office.

"This evening's decoy job's at Lingerie." She stuffed her hands into her jeans and moved from one foot to the other, her boots making a soft click on the floor.

Leo wondered how she'd handle that assignment. "Yeah. I thought Stacy and Denise would do well on that one. What do you think?"

She cleared her throat. "Lingerie's a lesbian club."

"I know." He waited for her to wrap her mind around his admission.

"They aren't gay."

"And?" He paused. "This is a job, an assignment requiring a different kind of role-playing. They aren't ready for this?"

She shook her head slowly. The overhead light glinted on strands of her short, dark hair and created shadows on one side of her face. Earnest, deep-set blue eyes regarded him. "Honestly, I don't know. I've been to this place several times and two young, attractive women will get hit on ... a lot."

"How is that different than when I send them to a bar where men hit on them? I'm thinking the procedure will be the same. They'll tape conversations with the target, not commit to anything, give the phone numbers and email addresses we've assigned, and move on. That's how I see the job. How do you see it?" During his comments her face reddened.

"That's how it should go, you're right. Do you mind if I ask them if they feel they can handle this assignment?"

Leo glanced at his watch. "Isn't that procedure for every job assignment?"

A tiny smile bloomed into a full grin. "Yes, of course. Sorry, I wasn't thinking. Just thought … well no matter, I'll take care of it." She turned and walked off.

"Barb."

She stopped and looked over her shoulder at him. He waved her into a chair and closed the door behind her.

"This works both ways." He needed to make his positions clear.

She frowned. "Huh?"

He straightened and held her gaze. "Exceptions can't be made for a person's sexuality and race, unless there could be complications. Nationality, gender … same thing about complications. I can't say this company doesn't discriminate against gays, or different races, or nationalities, and then don't assign jobs they can do if they blend in. Like I said, it works both ways."

He paused and watched as understanding flooded her gaze. "The only thing I took into consideration for this assignment was their ability to think on their feet and their gender. Now, if you don't think they can do the job, suggest someone else, but a decoy doesn't need to be gay to handle this job. Or straight to handle another. That's not something I'm going to do."

Her face reddened and she cleared her throat. "Thanks. Being gay, I appreciate that. And you're right, it works both ways."

"So what do you think? Can they do this or not?" he asked again ready to be done with this conversation.

"Yes, they're capable, and of course they can say no. I need to check for backups in case they do."

"Don't forget, each decoy provided hard limits on their applications. That's the list I used to make this assignment."

Her face relaxed and her eyes sparkled. "That's right. Damn, I'm forgetting everything today. Okay, so that job should be good. I'm with them at Lingerie."

Barb walked to the door, opened it, and looked at him. "Thanks for understanding. Few people mean what they say when it deals with the LGBT community. I've had lots of broken promises. Sometimes I over think things, make them more complicated."

"Yeah, you do, but it's part of your charm. Just keep the ladies out of trouble tonight and watch Mrs. Carter. Her husband wants more information."

There wasn't a whole lot more to say about the matter. Barb was a good person and employee no matter who she loved.

She nodded and left.

Leo sat behind his desk to check mail and search for components to create better electronic surveillance equipment. Last night's failure still bugged him. He couldn't understand why the scanner didn't work the first time.

Footsteps heading in his direction from the hall drew his attention. Derrick, a tall, black kid who'd been with him for two and a half years tapped on the open door.

"Can I talk to you for a minute?"

Leo nodded and turned off the monitor. "What's up?" His brow rose when Derrick closed the door and took a seat in the leather chair in front of his desk.

Derrick exhaled and then met Leo's gaze. "I need a favor."

"What kind of favor?" Working with college students, almost all favors were financial in some way. Although he'd been asked to write parental notes to professors, attend family gatherings as a date, contact parents to assure them his company was legitimate, but most favors involved money.

Derrick cleared his throat. "I'm short on cash and need some work. I know there's a system where you rotate us, but I really need to make some extra money."

Leo waited to see if Derrick would explain his emergency and when he didn't, Leo nodded and turned on the monitor. "I was just opening emails to see if there were any new jobs." His cell rang.

"Hold on, it's Cherise."

"Melinda Union is here. She needs to talk with you. She walked back there but your door's closed," she said.

"Yes, I'm meeting with Derrick. Tell her I need ten to fifteen minutes." He opened the company mail and saw three job requests from previous clients.

"She said she'll wait. It's about a job she needs done. Could be something Derrick could do," Cherise whispered.

Leo looked at Derrick and placed the call on mute. "There's a client out front with a new job. I can see if it's something you can do." The look of gratitude on Derrick's face intrigued him. *What had Derrick gotten himself into?* Chances are he'd never know.

"Man, I'd appreciate anything you can do." He stood. "I can wait while you talk to her."

"Okay. Wait in the conference room. I'll have Cherise send her back."

"Cool." Derrick's attitude leaving was ten times better than when he knocked hesitantly on the door a few minutes before. Leo hoped he could help him.

"Hello, Leo." Melinda walked with the confidence of someone in command of her life, certain of her abilities. Her lavender silky blouse dipped low in the front, accenting perfectly her dark suit, fair complexion, and long curly black hair.

He came around his desk. "How're you doing?" Leo took the hand she offered and shook it. Soft, yet strong.

Melinda was a woman of many contradictions, perhaps that was why he was attracted to her.

Her dark blue gaze met his with a smile. "Good, sorry for barging in, work has been crazy and this was the first break I've had. I appreciate you seeing me. I know you're busy, so I'll tell you what I need. Hopefully you can help me."

He moved back and waved to the leather chair Derrick recently vacated.

"I need you to follow this man." She slid a photo and two sheets of paper across the desk. "Twenty-four hours, around the clock, I want to know what he does, where he goes, who he's with—everything."

Leo looked at the photo, trying to place the face but couldn't. He glanced over the pages of information. "Dr. Bruce Wittier? Does he teach at the university?"

"No, he's a plastic surgeon. The best in the state," she said as if everyone knew about the man.

"How long do you want this done?" Leo asked gazing at the picture, silently admitting he had no idea who the man was but he'd fix that shortly.

"Four days. I need to know everything he does until the twenty-fifth. Complete anonymity, I'm doing this outside the firm. Have Cherise bill me directly. I'll leave a certified check for five thousand dollars as a retainer to get this started."

Leo's brow rose at the amount, and the fact she had it with her. "Tomorrow?"

Melinda hesitated and then nodded. "Tonight is better, if possible. Otherwise first thing in the morning when he goes to work. Take photos, videos, license plates, anything this man touches for the next four days I want a record of it."

"We can't follow him onto personal property," Leo reminded her.

"I know but everything else ... follow him."

"Is there any danger to our ops?" he asked.

Melinda's head snapped up with eyes narrowed and then she relaxed. "No, as far as I know there's no danger." Brow furrowed, she leaned forward looking much older than her twenty-eight years. "If the old boys at the top find out I'm looking at this guy, *my* job's in danger."

"Would you like an estimate, an idea of what we'll do?" he asked, keeping her personal or professional life out of the conversation.

She had done some legal work for him in the past when he started the company, but they didn't run in the same social circles and she *hadn't* cut him a deal when she worked for him. He would return the favor.

"Sure, what's the going rate for watching somebody 24-7?" She leaned back.

"Since you already understand the mechanics of surveillance, and understand that all my people do is observe, I'll skip the normal spiel."

"Thank you," Melinda said, her tone slightly sarcastic.

Leo grinned. Grit Inc. wasn't cheap, but they got results. "Someone will tail him in a car, and we'll have people on the ground if he's ever in a public place to record that as well. Depending on his office, I can have someone make an appointment to go see him, record him each day in his workplace to verify he's actually there."

"Excellent, I like that! Good thinking," Melinda said as if she didn't expect them to develop or utilize a game plan.

"After the first day, anything we think he'll repeat, we'll have people in place to record his actions so you can later observe his body language," Leo continued.

"Even better. Can I get daily reports rather than wait until the twenty-fifth?"

"Yes, but just until the initial retainer is exhausted, at that time you'll need to submit additional funds. Five thousand is a good start but for constant surveillance it will go fast. We pay our operatives promptly every week for services rendered that week," Leo said.

"Right. I'll leave this check and when my balance is at one thousand, send me a text and I'll send whatever Cherise says."

Ten minutes later, signed contract in hand Melinda left the office. Leo pulled out the keyboard and heard familiar footsteps followed by a knock on the door.

"Come in." Leo didn't turn. Instead, he focused on running a deep background check on the doctor. Something in the way Melinda acted bothered him. He wasn't sure what she expected this doctor to do or who he'd see, but Leo didn't want his people caught in any crossfire. If the doctor had a problem past, he wanted to know about it upfront.

"Anything?" Derrick asked, his voice full of hope.

"Yes, I think we may have something. I'm checking several databases for more information on the man she wants followed. This is a four-day surveillance job. How much time can you commit to it?"

"Nights, however long you need me," Derrick said, sitting forward in the chair.

"Eight's the max, I'll have you rotate with Griff and Barb. But you start tonight."

Derrick closed his eyes, his lips moved as if he were praying silently. "Thank you. Thank you so much." He stood, turned, and left the room.

Leo set up the account, sent Griff an email to report to work in the morning for the equipment he'd need before heading to the job. When it came to surveillance work, Leo used the same mounted cameras police officers used and remote stationary cameras that could be placed on rooftops if the target used the same place over and over. Those expensive devices were kept locked in the office.

Derrick tapped on the door again. Leo wasn't surprised when he closed the door behind him this time and stepped toward the desk. "Is there any way … any way I can get an advance on that? I wouldn't ask if it wasn't important, but it is."

Again, Leo waited for Derrick to share this emergency. When he didn't, Leo pulled out his calculator. "Four days, eight hours each day, at twenty bucks an hour."

Derrick nodded.

"I can give you half today." Leo looked up at Derrick, saw the relief cross his face, and hoped the college junior hadn't gotten into any trouble.

"That would be perfect. Leo, man you saved my life. Thanks so much. Anything you need I'm your guy. I mean that. Anything."

Leo smiled, entered the job in the computer and sent a request for a check to Cherise. "Give Cherise a couple minutes to take care of that. Keep it under your hat. I don't do that for everybody." Leo fist bumped Derrick.

"I know. I appreciate it." He headed to the door, a large grin split his face.

"Derrick?" Leo called.

"Yeah?" Derrick stuck his head back in the room.

"Tonight, 8:00 pm to 4:00 am shift. Eat, shit, love on your woman. Do all of that before your shift. We can't miss anything on this job."

Derrick smiled and then saluted him. "On it."

Chapter 3

Later that night, Leo leaned back in the chair, staring at the monitor, and waited for Barb to come online. Craig had an emergency at school, something to do with his thesis, and couldn't work tonight so Leo handled the console. Barb offered to cover for Craig, but Leo insisted she be onsite with Denise and Stacy since they were still relatively new to decoy work.

He glanced at the monitor to his left with the live feed from Derrick's surveillance gig. Barb had called the doctor's home number using one of their burner phones and hung up after the doctor told her she had the wrong number. Derrick verified the target was inside when he saw him through a window.

The center monitor flickered as Barb walked into Lingerie. Women, exquisitely beautiful women, were everywhere.

"Whoa." He leaned forward taking in the luscious view and then moved slightly to free up room in his tightening pants.

"Damn," he whispered as a tall, stacked brunette walked ahead of Barb and then turned left. Most men dreamed of being in a room filled with so many hot, sexy women, and he had a front seat. Granted, they wouldn't give him any play, but that didn't translate to body parts south.

"Give me ears," he spoke into the small mic in Barb's ear.

Seconds later a hip, sultry song flowed through the office sound system. He tried to recall the name of the popular tune by Beyoncé but couldn't. Off screen someone started a chorus of "Happy Birthday." Others joined in until it almost drowned out the music thumping through the speakers.

Female dancers on raised platforms wore skimpy bikinis, moving their hips in tune with the beat. Everyone seemed happy, having a great time. He'd never seen anything like this. How often did a man get the opportunity to see beautiful women without the pressure of finding the perfect combination of witty conversation and chemistry? Neither of those things would get him a serious date in that place, but he could enjoy the view and that made this assignment rock.

"This room reeks of toilet-water perfume, over-fried appetizers, and body odors with a hint of sex," Barb said.

Leo laughed. "As mic checks go, that was a good one."

"Pity you can't feel the music pulsing beneath my feet. I thought I'd fall on my ass walking over here." She made her way to the bar. Several friends waved and called out to her. Barb ordered a beer from Nicky, the bartender. The two seemed to know each other.

"We need to hire some of their staff as E&Es. Give out some of your business cards if you have them with you."

"Will do. That would've helped some tonight."

When a corner seat at the bar became available, Barb moved, pulled out her phone, and turned on the Grit App. A larger live feed of the club filled the monitor on Leo's right. Tonight he'd use three monitors for this job and then edit them so the client could see his wife from a variety of angles.

For this assignment each decoy received special phones for live feed recording, email addresses, and burner numbers to give the target or anyone who asked for ways to get in touch later. Under no circumstances could the decoys share personal information that the target could trace. At the end of the night they'd turn in the phones and retrieve their personal devices from the office.

Leo grabbed a cup of coffee and settled into his seat. The client wanted information on his wife's extracurricular activities with women. Mr. Carter hadn't seemed bothered by his wife's affairs when he hired Grit Inc, and claimed he simply wanted proof. By the end of the night they'd have it.

Stacy and Denise seemed excited over the job and asked Barb pertinent questions on how to act in the club and around their target, Mrs. Carter. After answering their questions, Barb spent half an hour demonstrating how to use the equipment and testing their mics. Not once did they seem bothered by spending the next few hours with women who would try to take them home or into the bathroom for a quickie. Leo appreciated their flexibility.

"Hey, haven't seen you in a while," a cute brunette said. Leo hadn't seen her approach and gave her a quick once over.

"Same here. How you been, Ginger?" Barb asked after setting her phone in a position so the camera covered the entrance.

Stacy and Denise would arrive separately and work the room independent of the other, which seemed the best strategy. After seeing pictures of both decoys, Mr. Carter was sure his wife would be attracted to Stacy, but wanted her to see sexy Denise as well.

Ginger twirled a few strands of her hair around her finger while watching Barb. "Lonely. What about you?"

Barb cleared her throat. "I'm good, busy."

Leo turned down the volume to give Barb privacy and his ears a break from the loud music.

Ginger's smile faltered. "Busy? You've met someone?"

"Of course, didn't you?"

"Well, I … not really. It's been a while since we've spent time together," Ginger said.

Leo hummed to drown out the conversation while watching the screen. He stopped when Denise walked in wearing a black, skin-tight, sleeveless dress that showcased her shape and youth to perfection. Her dark hair flowed around her shoulders, displaying a smooth, heart-shaped face and light brown eyes. Leo smiled at the contacts Denise wore and wondered if Stacy also altered her appearance. "Very nice."

Ginger turned and looked at Denise. "Is that your new flavor?"

Leo heard the disbelief in Ginger's voice and disliked her immediately. If she and Barb had real history, he hoped it remained in the past.

"No, but she's hot," Barb said with a smidgeon of pride.

Ginger walked off in a huff.

"She looks amazing. Are there any other black women in there?" He turned the volume up a bit while watching Denise.

"Not many but it's still early," Barb answered.

Denise walked around as if on a runway. Her glance skidded past Barb and then she moved to a table not too far away. She pulled out her phone as if checking messages. Seconds later her image was live.

She winked at him and tapped her ear.

"Let me just say, I cannot believe the awesome amount of beautiful women in that place with you ladies tonight. You are indeed a first-class diamond," he told her.

"Thank you," Denise said. Now that she'd turned on her device, he activated the small camera in her necklace and focused on the room.

"The target is sitting on the sofa near the party," Barb said and turned her phone in that direction.

Denise moved her chair so that she faced Mrs. Carter. The woman now appeared on two screens.

"She doesn't seem happy," Barb said.

Denise gasped.

"What is it?" Leo asked looking at all the monitors for problems.

"Ms. Jackson. Stephanie Jackson, my English Lit professor she's sitting at that table talking to the redhead. Oh shit."

"You think there might be some trouble? She might say something that'll give away what you're doing? Or cause problems for you at school?" Leo stared at the nice looking brunette with long wavy hair and killer bod. She laughed at something the red head said displaying a dimple in one cheek and even white teeth.

"I don't know, I just hope she doesn't hit on me. That would be awkward."

"I'll let Barb know and she'll run interference, if things get ... awkward as you say I'll pull you out. Stacy should be there soon, wanna call her and give her a heads up?"

Denise sighed and straightened her back. "No. We'll deal with whatever happens, I just didn't expect to see a teacher or so many women here. I'm kinda scared to look around, who knows who else I might see."

"If you don't think you can do this, tell me and I'll have Barb get you out of there," he said watching both screens.

"No, it just surprised me that's all. I didn't know she was... that she preferred women. Give me a second to get back in character."

Leo smiled. "Okay. If you change your mind, just let me know."

Denise's red dot flashed on the screen.

"Hello," a low, well-modulated voice said to Denise.

"Hello." Denise said.

"May I buy you a drink?" An older white female sat in the chair next to Denise.

"Yes, a Long Island Ice Tea please."

"I told you," Barb murmured.

Fascinated, Leo listened as this older woman flirted with Denise. Fortunately everything was recorded. He'd need to go back and take notes because she was damn good.

Ten minutes later Stacy strode into the room wearing black tight jeans and midriff top, black boots, bangles, heavy makeup, and her hair pulled back in a ponytail. She looked like a dominatrix without the whip.

Barb squeaked and then laughed.

Leo stared in surprise at the decoys interpretation of this assignment. Both were sexy as hell, but different as night and day. If Mrs. Carter didn't spill the beans tonight to one of them, she wasn't human. From the moment Denise, and later Stacy, walked into the club, they drew a lot of attention. Women walked past them and stopped to look back. Some turned in their chairs, checking Stacy out as she stopped and talked to a short woman that Barb had said owned the club.

From what he could see, there weren't many black women in the club and certainly none as young and hot as Denise. The older woman continued flirting. Denise dodged most of her questions, answering only a few.

Leo lowered the volume on Denise and focused on Stacy, who grabbed the attention of a younger, wilder crowd. Mrs. Carter sat near that group watching and occasionally laughing. Every now and then a slender, young woman with long blond hair would pull away from the dance floor and snuggle against Carter. Barb took a few pictures from her vantage point at the bar. He hoped Stacy did better.

"Do we know who the young woman is that keeps talking to Mrs. Carter?" Leo asked.

"Not yet," Stacy said.

Ms. Jackson noticed Stacy and walked to her.

"Oh, oh she's talking to Stacy and holding her arm," Barb said moving in that direction.

Ms. Jackson turned, noticed Denise and then glanced at Stacy again. A few minutes later she left the club.

Stacy plopped into the empty seat near Mrs. Carter and they started talking. When the young woman visited Mrs. Carter the next time, she stood looking down at them. Neither Stacy nor Mrs. Carter moved.

"They seem to be doing fine. You worried for nothing, mama bear," Leo said, teasing Barb.

"You're right. They're naturals at this." Barb moved to the bar.

"Give me a beer." The blonde who'd been with Carter earlier stood next to Barb. She looked over her shoulder in the direction of Stacy and Mrs. Carter. "I was getting tired of her anyway," she muttered.

"Yeah?"

She turned and looked down at Barb. "Lillian."

"Barb."

Lillian nodded and took her beer.

Barb signaled the bar tender to put the beer on her tab.

"Thank you," Lillian said and took another pull. "That's good." She met Barb's glance. "I'm not free, and although I appreciate the beer, there's nothing I do that only costs a beer."

Leo coughed and almost fell from his chair. "What the hell?" He hadn't seen that coming. Prostitutes? Call Girls? Mrs. Carter? How would Mr. Carter feel about that?

"No worries. The beer's just because you're pretty. You don't owe me anything. Somebody having a birthday party?" she asked.

Lillian fingered a gaudy looking necklace with a large green stone surrounded by smaller ones and then took another drink. "Yes, it's my birthday."

Barb lifted her glass and clinked Lillian's. "Happy birthday, pretty lady."

"Thanks, that's really nice of you." She finished off her drink, pushed back, and returned to the crowded section.

"She's a pro, you know that right?" the bartender asked.

"She mentioned it," Barb said. "Interested in more work?" she asked.

"Sure, as long as it's above board."

Barb slid her card across the bar. Nicky looked at it, stuck it in her pocket, and walked off.

For the next hour and a half, Stacy sat and talked with Carter. Lillian eventually sat at the table with Denise and an older woman who'd occupied a large part of her time.

Leo recorded everything. Too many conversations went on at once. He muted the sound and watched the four screens.

"Derrick, you with me?" Leo asked and glanced at the clock. Derrick came on at eight and worked until four. Griff would relieve him at four and work until noon.

"Yeah, I've been transmitting every hour. You copied any of that?"

Leo checked the quality of the downloaded files. "Got them. Nothing much, but she wanted everything."

"As long as the client's happy," Derrick said.

"And paying for you to sit outside and watch him sleep," Leo said, watching Stacy on the sofa with the target and Denise on the dance floor. He got a closer look at Lillian and took a snapshot for the client.

"True, so very true," Derrick said.

"Denise still scheduled to leave first?" Barb asked, signaling to Stacy to wrap things up.

"Yes, then Stacy, and then you." Leo looked at the financial clock. They had wiggle room, but he needed to complete edits which would eat into the rest of the client's fee significantly.

Barb squeaked as a hand landed on her shoulder. Leo smiled. He'd seen Denise walk in Barb's direction.

"Hi, I'm Niecey. Why're you sitting here by yourself?" Denise asked, drawing the eyes of everyone nearby.

"No reason," Barb said, her voice hesitant.

"Come dance with me." Denise's eyes twinkled as she held out her hand.

Leo noticed interest in the eyes of a few women who hadn't paid Barb attention before and wanted to kiss Denise.

Barb placed her recorder into her pocket, took Denise's hand, and walked to the dance floor.

"Don't laugh. I've got two left feet," Barb muttered. Dressed in her customary jeans, a red long-sleeved shirt, which she'd pushed up her forearm and dark boots, she looked like she'd rather be anywhere but there.

"Me too, so cut a rug for both of us," Leo said, smiling as Barb rocked from side to side and Denise danced in tune with the beat.

The song ended and another started. Denise leaned close and whispered into Barb's ear, "I was offered a job as a call girl."

Chapter 4

Tell Barb about the call girl stuff," Stacy told Denise as they walked down the hall toward the training room to fill out their reports and retrieve their personal phones. The clack of their heels heard above their constant chatter.

Leo stepped into the hall and offered a fist bump to each of them. Stacy mimicked cracking a whip. He laughed and pointed to their outfits. "Way to go. Tonight had to be the most entertaining evening I've had in a long time." He bowed from his waist. "Thank you ladies, you were excellent."

"They did good, really good," Barb agreed, catching up with them.

"Did you hear this, Barb?" Stacy asked when Barb and Leo entered the room. "That older lady was talking to her about selling her services to both men and women."

"I didn't get all the details," Barb said. "First, write up your reports and make sure you've uploaded your recordings and pictures."

Stacy's long conversation with Mrs. Carter had been taped, but it was still important to relay the facts as they recalled.

"Yeah. I did that before I got in my car," Denise said, sitting at the computer.

"Me too," Stacy added. For the next few minutes, keyboards clacked in the silence.

A sense of pride filled Leo over how well the recent jobs had gone. Despite his fears, the company survived the first two years and helped people. These two pre-law students were an excellent example. Eager to hear Denise's job proposition he waited silently in the chair.

"Done." Stacy turned in her chair and watched Denise.

Barb pulled up the report, read Stacy's comments, and placed her signature in the appropriate space.

"Me too." Denise leaned back in her chair, watching as Barb reviewed the report.

"Okay, now that that's done, I gotta say I love how you ladies worked tonight." Barb waved at them. "Your outfits, attitude, everything just worked. Let me take your pictures."

Laughing, Denise and Stacy jumped up and did a Charlie's Angels pose.

"That'd make a good poster to go in this room for future trainees," Leo told Barb.

"Yeah, that's a great idea."

"Dressing like this was Stacy's idea," Denise said. "She wanted to get into character and went all Goth."

"Goth? I thought dominatrix," Barb said, looking at Stacy's outfit again.

Stacy's face reddened and her mouth dropped open.

Leo smothered a laugh.

Denise held her stomach and laughed until tears rolled down her cheeks. When she could speak, she pointed at Stacy. "I … I told you."

Smiling, Stacy cleared her throat and pulled on the edge of her midriff top. "Yeah, you did. But it worked. That Carter lady is really miserable. She never should've married her husband. Claims she only did it because of her parents. She's got a long story, but I think she's been cheating on him from day one."

"He's probably doing the same thing," Denise said, wiping her eyes and crossing her legs.

"But he's the client. Wonder why he wants to know what women his wife messes with?" Stacy asked.

"Who knows?" Denise said. "I think we have enough information to satisfy Mr. Carter." She looked at Barb. "That was fun. At first I wasn't sure how I'd feel with other women trying to talk to me, but they respected my boundaries and nobody pushed. Wasn't bad at all."

Barb smiled and glanced at Leo, who gave her his "told you so" look.

"Not bad at all. If half the jobs we went on had men who talked in long, cohesive sentences like Mrs. Carter, I wouldn't feel sorry for their wives or whoever wants to know what they're doing while in town." Stacy looked at Barb. "Really, some of those guys are just dogs. Their wives have to know they're cheating—"

"Or trying to cheat," Denise said. "The only time I understood why the woman wanted to know what the man was up to was that case when the girlfriend hired decoys to see how her boyfriend acted around other women."

"Woof, woof," Stacy barked. "He acted like a dog. But she was the other woman, right?"

Leo nodded, remembering that case clearly. The girlfriend had been waiting five years for the guy to leave his wife. She dumped him after receiving their report.

"Not all the guys are bad." Stacy smiled. "One job I met a doctor—"

"He wasn't the target, his best friend was," Denise said. "Both of them talked to you, didn't that ring a bell? Can we say ménage?"

Stacy's face reddened. "Well, that might've been interesting." She glanced at Leo. "Company policy forbids contact with targets before or after the job, I know. But he was cute—"

"And old enough to be your dad ..." Denise added in a dry tone.

"Yeah, there's that. Anyway, tonight was fun, nice mixing the jobs up. Plus, I can use the money."

"True. Nice way to spend a Saturday night, dancing at a club and making a couple hundred bucks legally." Denise laughed.

"And you got some action," Stacy said, pointing at Barb. "I saw you with the lady at the bar when I was leaving."

Leo looked at Barb, her face turned red.

"Really?" Denise raised her brow as a large smile formed on her face. "Which one? Red or green?"

"Green blouse," Barb said.

Leo hadn't a clue.

"Good, she'd been eyeing you most of the night," Denise said, surprising Barb.

"Yeah and there was another one. I think she had on a blue dress," Stacy said, snapping her fingers as she talked.

Leo stood and stretched to draw the attention away from Barb. He could tell she grew uneasy with the discussion. "I'm proud of you, ladies, your work was impeccable."

"Thanks, boss." Denise saluted him.

"So are you going into private practice as a call girl?" Stacy asked Denise.

Denise winked. "Lillian said it paid big bucks and perks. She was wearing a banging necklace an old lover gave her. She only tricks with women, though. The old bird, the madam … I can't remember her name, it sounded foreign, said I could pick my clients."

"Clients? Is that what they're calling them these days?" Stacy laughed.

"Yep, here's the thing. Mrs. Carter is a client. She's a regular. Lillian was the tenth girl she'd used. Pays over two hundred dollars an hour."

Leo stopped smiling. *Did she say over two hundred an hour?*

Stacy stopped laughing and whistled. "You're shitting me?"

"Nope, that's what Madam told me and then called Lillian over to verify. Lillian graduated last year with a master's degree in psychology, I think. Anyway, she's working this to pay off her college loans and then plans to return home to Michigan. Based on what she told me, she's got a lot going for her."

"Plus tricking with women you don't run the risk of getting pregnant," Stacy said.

"True." Denise and Stacy slapped each other's palms.

"So you're interested?" Leo asked Denise, unsure by the tone of the conversation.

"No. The whole idea of getting paid for something I think is really special doesn't appeal to me…" she tapped her forehead "…and I'll make money using this."

"Heard that," Stacy said and then looked at Leo. "Ask me."

He laughed, guessing from her bouncing up and down on the seat what her answer would be. "Are you going into private practice as a call girl?"

"For two hundred dollars an hour? Hell yeah, as long as I can bring my whip." She stood, made a motion as if cracking a whip, then placed her booted foot on the chair. "Make him my boy toy, have him bring me a sandwich when I study, and drive me to my decoy assignments."

They all laughed at her antics.

"You are not well," Denise said, standing and walking toward the door. "It's time for you to take off those tight boots. They're making you think strange things."

Stacy pouted and then laughed. "You're killing my buzz." She waved at Barb and Leo and then followed Denise.

Chapter 5

A few days later, Saturday night Leo monitored the console for a few hours after returning from a dateless night in the movie theater. Granted the sci-fi was one he'd wanted to see since it came out last week but it sucked he hadn't thought far enough in advance to ask Barb if she'd like to go. Derrick's red dot, as the sole decoy working that night, stood prominently in a sea of blue dots.

Leo activated the nightly scan of Ghost, the hardware and software system he created to run his company. The closed system allowed limited internet access and only accepted images and videos from the app he created specifically to work in tandem with Ghost. Even though chances of viruses from the app were slim since each E&E person was activated as needed, he remained vigilant in protecting his programs. A well learned lesson from when he created Venom.

"You awake, Derrick?"

"Yeah, listening to music, got my eyes on the doc."

During the past few days the doctor retired at a 6:00 pm and then left his home around three in the morning to head to a warehouse on the opposite side of town near Research Park, where he remained until 6:00 am. So far, no one joined him, and they had no idea what the man did for three hours every morning. Melinda had been surprised by their report, but grateful. She had no idea what he did in there either.

"Both days I've tracked him to that warehouse. First night I placed a small camera on top of a twenty-foot shipping container. It's holding well. I see most of the place without being on the property."

"Good deal."

"Think he's going back to the warehouse?" Leo took a sip of hot coffee and leaned back.

"When I left yesterday he was still there. Griff said he stays until six, goes home, and leaves for his office around nine."

"Yep, that's what he wrote in the report," Leo said. "Tomorrow's the last day shadowing the doctor, and no one has any idea what the man does in that warehouse."

"Nope, not a clue. You won't let us look around during our off time to get answers."

"That's not what we were hired to do. Surveillance. Plain and simple. Watch and report. That's it. Seriously. Don't over step on this," Leo said, hardening his voice.

"Got it. Doc's strange, but it's not our business. Glad this is the last day, though got some things I need to handle," Derrick said.

"Yeah? Everything okay?" Etiquette was a tricky thing, there's a fine line between showing concern and being a nosy SOB. Leo hated these situations and preferred when people simply said what was on their minds without him asking questions.

"Yeah... it's cool."

Relieved he didn't need to go any further he stood, prepared to call it a night.

"Pam's pledging a sorority this semester, and doesn't want her family to know."

"Oh, okay." He sat back down and turned up the volume.

"Which would be cool except they'd have a fit if they knew she spent a part of her allowance for pledge fees and came up short."

Ah, the reason Derrick worked the extra hours. "Is it expensive?" Leo had never pledged in college. He'd applied during his sophomore year but had been rejected and didn't bother after that.

"Extremely. Well for a college student on financial aid and no family support, it's real expensive," Derrick said, his tone rising on the end, sounding more alive than before.

"Well… I'm sure things will work out." Leo shook his head at his lame response but had no idea what to say. He'd only met Pam once last year at a holiday get together at a local bar, she seemed nice. Derrick liked her. What else could he say?

Derrick snorted. "It better, I'm getting tired of being alone all the time. When I'm off she's either with her pledge group or classes. She doesn't have any time for much else, a brother got needs, know what I'm saying?"

"Definitely, most definitely," Leo said immediately, totally understanding and then tried to recall the last time he had his needs met.

"It's wild how this thing's taking over so much of her life, but she says it's almost done. They go over next week."

"Go over?"

"Finish pledging, she promised to make it up to me. I've planned a weekend in the mountains."

"Mountains? That sounds great. I should take notes from you, Pam's going to be really happy."

"Not as happy as I'll be to have her alone, you feel me?"

"Yeah." Leo grinned. Had he ever had a one track mind like that? He didn't think so, maybe that's why he sat in his office on a Saturday night working instead of making plans for a hot, sexy weekend with a woman.

"Should be sweet. I need that weekend off by the way."

Leo typed in the request, verified the date and wished Derrick the best before heading to his office. After reviewing a few case files, he left for home. Tomorrow would knock on the door of time soon enough. He said goodnight to Derrick, reminded him to upload his photos hourly, and went home.

Melinda called first thing the next morning after receiving updates to thank him for the great job. She still remained in the dark regarding her client's activities, but time had run out and she needed to represent him in court.

Mr. Carter hadn't been happy with his wife's activities, but he'd been pleased with their services. He'd been sure Mrs. Carter would try to pick up Stacy and seemed disappointed when informed his wife hadn't called or sent an email. Carter hinted he made need to hire them again, but didn't make a solid commitment and Leo didn't push beyond a customary, "we're here to help."

Three jobs came in. One from Thompson, who'd hired them to identify Phelps. Leo read the job: keep Nolan Green in the bar for thirty minutes. That was it. He re-read the order, signed off on the contract, and returned it by secure email. Stacy and Denise would handle it if they were available. Thompson sent a short personal note as well. The contents intrigued Leo. He printed the job orders and note and headed to Barb's office.

Craig, the other techie in the office, sat in the computer room retrofitting cameras and mics into necklaces, bracelets, even rings for the male decoys. Leo nodded at him as he passed, glad to see the grad student back at work.

"I've got these two jobs." He handed Barb the pages and sat on the corner of her desk.

"Put Derrick on the surveillance? It's one day," she said

"Sounds good." Derrick's paperwork and files were perfect. He utilized the equipment with great skill, making it easy for Leo or Craig to manipulate the data and send crisp reports to their clients.

She bit her lip looking at the next one. It required a female to work in a boutique for a week to watch the target the owner suspected of stealing.

"Hmm, we need an older decoy for this one, don't you think?" She looked at him and then back at the page.

"Define older. I'm twenty-eight, you're twenty-five. Are we in the older category?"

She laughed, her smile brightening dark blue eyes with tiny wrinkles at the corners. "Other than Cherise and compared to everyone who works here, we're old and almost decrepit."

"Never decrepit," he said with a straight face before smiling. "Something came in today for our wonder twins, Ebony and Ivory. They play well off each other, makes them stronger."

Barb nodded. "They've been roommates since their freshman year and are like sisters. If you take on one, you got both of them coming at you. Can you imagine their future law firm? It'll be seriously kick-ass." She looked at the paper again. "I'll give Stephanie a call to see if she's available. This might be perfect for her."

Leo nodded, remembering the young preppy blonde who'd graduated last year. He didn't know she remained in the area. "Look at this." He handed her the note from Mr. Thomas.

She read it and then met his gaze. "He wants you to go to a bid conference for a government contract? To do what … jobs like we're doing now?"

He shrugged. "I didn't look up the RFP." He shook his head at her frown. "Request for Proposal."

Understanding flooded her gaze. Somehow Grit, Inc., Leo's small North Carolina network, had captured the notice of a government organization. While he appreciated the extra work, he wasn't sure about this whole contract thing, especially if they did deep background checks.

"I didn't look it up yet to get the scope of the work, but he thinks this is something we can do." Leo wondered what she thought. Thompson hadn't been a client long. Seemed strange he'd make this recommendation without knowing the company's full capabilities.

Her eyes lit as her smile widened. "That would be blockbuster grand. We can do it."

He laughed. "Hold on there, speedy. We don't know what *it* is, but it does feel good to be invited to the party."

She wagged her finger at him. "Somebody's watching you."

He captured her finger and squeezed before letting it go. "Us. They're watching us. Our network, our team."

Barb punched her fist in the air. "Decoy University!"

Leo laughed at the nickname she'd given the network and turned when he heard footsteps.

Cherise walked in holding a large envelope. "This was just delivered. I signed for it." Frowning she looked up at him. "It's from a lawyer."

"Thank you." He took the manila envelope and headed to his office, opening it along the way. The words on the page stopped him cold. Someone was suing him, the company, and a decoy, who worked for him last year, for entrapment.

"Entrapment?" He read the charge again, trying to remember the case. Moving quickly to his desk he signed into the separate server which housed all of his past case files and employee records. From the day he started business until now he kept every record.

"*Orion Brewer*." He typed in the name, waited a few seconds for the file to appear, and then read the report.

"Son of a bitch. Entrapment my ass," Leo murmured, watching the video of Brewer following Amy, a petite, curvy decoy, the moment she entered the bar, begging her to talk to him. She gave him the company provided phone number. Leo looked at the records showing the number of times Brewer called, left messages, and shook his head. Regardless of how baseless the claim was, Leo had to respond.

He called Melinda and made an appointment for later that day.

Chapter 6

"Based on the detailed information you've shown me, Mr. Brewer doesn't have a case," Melinda said looking at one of the pages that proved Brewer made several attempts to contact the decoy after the initial meeting. "Entrapment is typically used in criminal cases against law enforcement officers accused of enticing a person to commit some type of crime they wouldn't normally commit. It's a stretch to use in the private sector. Even if a leap could be made, which is doubtful, the video clearly shows Mr. Brewer approached the decoy and his continued attempts to gain her attention even after she blew him off twice. He asked for her phone number and email address, which she gave. There's no indication she set him up or offered any information to get back in touch with him."

Before Leo started using decoys, he'd hired an attorney to advise him of the law and loopholes. The lawyer who created his E&E, decoy, and employee contracts had retired and moved away last year. But he had been very clear on what could and couldn't be done.

"Thanks, that's what I thought. I'd like to hire you to answer this complaint and represent me if we go to court."

Melinda smiled. "Certainly. I'll start by contacting his attorney. This is so far out in left field I'm thinking something else must be going on." She looked at her watch. "I'll call him now, if you have a few minutes."

Relieved to get started on putting this to rest, he nodded. "Sure. I'd appreciate that."

While she made the call, he looked around her small office. The office was painted beige, with one floor-to-ceiling window looking into another building. On the desk sat a laptop, and two stacks of papers, one much smaller than the other. A bookshelf, bare of books and filled with knickknacks was in a corner, beneath an ornate framed degree. The whole place lacked warmth and personalization. Had she just moved in or planned to move out?

"Mr. Grit is in my office and has no intention of allowing Mr. Brewer anywhere near the young lady." She inhaled and shook her head.

A few moments later she met his gaze and winked. "Go ahead; I've seen the videotape of what happened that night. This case is no more than your client trying to reconnect with a woman he met. Believe me, I'll let the courts know that when I present the evidence of what really happened that night."

Leo exhaled and looked out the window behind Melinda. At Barb's badgering, he'd researched the RFP before leaving the office. They'd both agreed it was a stretch to meet all the requirements but with proper planning it could be done. Since no one, other than his two past room-mates, knew he created Venom, Leo weighed the risks of exposure in light of Barb's absolute confidence of them winning the multi-million dollar bid.

The contract spanned seven states but allowed a liberal amount of time to open new offices, so that wasn't too much of an issue. He'd need to advertise on the college campuses, set up satellite offices. The company could handle cyber security and intelligence, but not armed security or surveillance. Those would be subcontracted to another vendor.

Barb wanted him to go to the bid conference and suggested a security company she'd heard of for parts of the contract they weren't qualified to handle. The challenge of expanding Ghost to operate efficiently in several states appealed to him on a gut level. Even though he'd covered his tracks the knowledge that others would dig into his life blunted his motivation.

Melinda disconnected.

He looked at her. "Well?"

She smiled. "He's going to talk to his client, explain the matter. They didn't think you had such thorough records from that night. After I told him what his client wore and gave descriptive facts regarding the large ring on his right hand, his attorney backed off. If they go any further with this, I'll let you know."

"Excellent." Leo stood and paused. "Would you like to have dinner with me?" His stomach clenched. He wasn't sure why he asked her out, but now that he had and she hadn't told him to go jump off a bridge, he'd run with it.

"Sure." Smiling, she pushed back and stood. "Let me get a few things together and we can leave." She took a few steps and looked at him over her shoulder. "Does this have anything to do with work or is this personal?"

He dragged his gaze from her round ass back to her eyes. "Personal for me."

"Good, give me a second." She walked out leaving a trail of her perfume behind.

Leo rocked on the heels of his shoes, grateful she'd said yes and pleased to spend time with someone smart and sexy, a potent combination. He released a long stream of air, glad to have that Brewer situation under control and happy he'd driven his car instead of the truck.

Melinda returned. "Ready?"

"Yes." He walked behind her and they took the elevator. "There's a French restaurant that I eat at on occasion. Do you like French food?"

Twenty minutes later they sat Chez Pala, named after the chef and owner. The restaurant was full, not surprising for this time of evening when the seniors tried to beat the rush and get a discount. Relatively close to downtown, several tables were full with people who preferred to wait for the traffic to die down. Leo loved the Coquilles Saint-Jacques and Sole Meniere and ordered the same dish each time. Melinda ordered the Bouillabaisse but looked at the menu as if she'd lick the pictures of some of the prepared dishes. He'd never understand why women didn't just eat and ride a bike or walk to deal with the calories later. The waiter recommended a nice crisp white wine and they were set.

Melinda took a sip and moaned. "Excellent."

Leo took his first sip and agreed. "My grandmother was French and loved to cook. I loved visiting her and Papa. Every time I come here, it reminds me of them." He took another sip and fiddled with the stem of his glass as he replayed what he'd just shared.

"My first taste of French cuisine happened on a summer trip my roommate and I took one summer during college." Melinda's brow furrowed. "Between junior and senior year I believe. I fell in love with the old buildings, the unhurried lifestyle, and the food." She laughed and he appreciated how it reached her eyes, making her appear much younger.

"And all the walking. We walked everywhere and had a great time. I'd like to go back one day, maybe stay longer and see some of the historical sites. We spent most of our time exploring the nightlife." She grinned.

"It's a lot of fun. I've been several times and there's nothing like the countryside. It's beautiful, can't get a decent signal, but other than that worthy of a daytrip at least," he said as memories of family trips or vacations coalesced in his mind. His grandparents would return every year and stay for a month, sometimes two, before returning.

"Sounds great, I'll put that on my bucket list."

Leo raised his glass.

She tapped his.

"Here's to fun places to see and explore."

"Amen to that." She took a healthy sip. The waiter refilled their glasses and then served the first course of soup.

"Leo," the masculine voice called from across the room.

"Zeke." Leo stood, smiling at his friend and former roommate. They embraced and bumped fists. "When did you get back in town? Last time we talked you took an assignment in Alexandria."

"Right. Got an offer in the Triangle I couldn't refuse, so I'm back." Zeke looked at Melinda and nodded. "Hello, sorry to interrupt your meal, just wanted to say hi to my homeboy. We go all the way back to high school."

"Zeke this is Melinda, Melinda … Zeke."

Melinda smiled and nodded. "Nice to meet you, even better knowing Leo was a youngster once."

Leo wagged his finger at her, liking this side of her personality.

She laughed.

"You still at your place?" Zeke asked Leo.

"Yeah, man, stop by sometime. Let's catch up," Leo said, truly happy to see him. They'd gotten into a lot of stuff back then, most of it illegal now. But they'd been solid.

Zeke handed him his card. "Cool. Here's my number. Enjoy your dinner, good seeing you."

"Same here." He placed the card in his wallet and watched the big guy walk away.

"He seems nice," Melinda said after Leo returned to his seat.

"He's a good guy." Zeke's dares had been the catalyst for most of Leo's better creations. He'd never been good at losing.

"So what do you think the doctor's been doing in that warehouse for three hours every day the past four days?" she asked into the silence.

Leo's brow rose at the change of topic. "I don't know."

"No, I know you don't know, but what do you think?"

Leo met her direct gaze and wondered if the wine had loosened her up. "Hmm, never gave it any thought. Maybe he's building something personal."

Her eyes widened and then she blinked a few times. One of her eyes was dark blue, the other dark gray. The difference was slight but staring at her, he noticed.

"Never gave it any thought?" She took a healthy swallow of wine. "It's consumed me."

He couldn't imagine why.

"I've wondered what made him leave home in the wee hours of the morning and drive so far to a warehouse."

Leo's brow rose as she repeated herself. He looked at her empty wine glass just as the waiter refilled it. He ordered another bottle, curious to meet the real Melinda Union.

"I went there at lunchtime the second day."

"Really?" Leo never mentioned the remote camera Derrick had placed on the grounds or that recorded twenty-four hours a day before they removed it this afternoon. As far as he knew, no one ever reviewed the feed when the doctor wasn't there, so her secret was safe.

"Yeah." She pushed the dark strands brushing against her face behind her ear. "Locked, couldn't get in."

"Probably best, you don't want to know—"

"Yes, I do want to know." She looked around and then leaned forward. "He's gone through every attorney in the firm, no one wants him as a client, so of course he winds up on my desk." She rolled her eyes. "I had to represent him this morning." She waved her hand. "Simple case. But he wouldn't cooperate with me. Me, his attorney." She slapped her chest, lightly drawing his eyes to her full breasts, reminding him of the women at Lingerie.

Leo placed a large spoonful of soup in his mouth to keep it closed.

"Anyway, I just wanted to know what made him so toxic as a client. If Graves, one of the partners, wasn't his brother-in-law, this wouldn't be an issue."

"True." Leo didn't care one way or the other, but he assumed she needed him to appear to listen and offer a positive remark.

The waiter removed their bowls and served his Coquilles Saint-Jacques and her shrimp cocktail.

"Try this, you'll love it." He held up his plate offering her a spoonful.

"Oh, smells delicious, thank you." She placed one on her small plate and took a bite. "This is yummy." She cleaned his fork before using her fork to take a little more. "So, Leo can I ask you a personal question?"

"Only if I can ask you one." He'd learned the correct response to that question several years ago when he'd gone to social outings with a few friends. Usually it stopped people from asking whatever they'd planned.

"Fair enough," she said then looked at him. "I know you've never been married or engaged and that you prefer women and you're really smart with a higher government clearance than me."

Shock raced through him, robbing him of speech. He leaned back in his chair staring at her. How'd she know about his government clearance?

"My question is this: do you want children?"

"What?" He couldn't wrap his mind around her question. "Children?"

"Well not do you want any per se, but have you ever considered participating in ... well a pregnancy?"

He looked at her empty glass and the second half-empty bottle of wine and relaxed. "No, not yet. Have you?"

"That was so good, may I have some more of that?" Her fork was poised over his plate.

"Sure." He moved the plate closer so she could take another.

"You can have some of my shrimp." She pushed the chilled glass with the shrimp on the rim toward him.

"No thank you, this is fine. Answer my question, have you considered children?" he asked, still surprised at the strange question.

She ate a bite while nodding. "Yes, quite often actually."

Uncertain how much of her plans he wanted to know, he finished his coquilles in silence.

"Do you think you'll ever have children?" she asked, splintering the quiet.

Since he wasn't dating, or particularly interested in bringing children into his life at the moment, he shrugged. "Maybe one day."

"Smart, good way to think about it." She paused. "Are you dating anyone?"

"No. You?"

"No. Workaholics don't usually make good dates."

He smiled. "True."

Grinning, she pointed at him. "You're one ... a workaholic. What are you working on now?" She leaned forward.

He looked up at her and then answered, "Trying to decide if I want to submit a RFP for government work."

Her smile faded as she held his gaze. "Really?"

Not the reaction he expected, but he nodded. "Yes, a client sent me the information, wants me to attend a bid conference."

"Big contract?" Her voice was now strong, sober.

"I'm not sure of all the particulars, but it's in the millions. Why?"

For the first time that night she picked up her water glass and drank. "Before I took this job at Miller, Brown, and Graves, I worked at a law firm in Atlanta. One of my cases was a small business who went after a large government contract. It took him a while to find other small contractors to help fulfill the requirements, but he did and submitted the bid."

She took another long drink and stared at the table for a few minutes. The waiter served their main courses, and she never returned to the topic. A part of him wanted to know what happened, did they win the contract or not. Another part of him didn't want to be influenced by anything. He'd prefer to make up his own mind.

When they finished the meal, she reached across the table and placed her hand on top of his, drawing his attention.

"Be careful. When it comes to large million-dollar contracts, the rules change even though they appear the same. The companies that win those contracts do everything within their power to keep them. They're quite ruthless sometimes." Her gaze radiated sincerity.

"Thank you. I haven't decided if I'm going to the conference to learn more about it yet, but if I go, I promise I'll be careful. I won't introduce myself or talk about my company, it'll just be to gather information."

Chapter 7

Barb hadn't let up until Leo rsvp'd to attend the bid conference to get more information and was all too happy with her punishment of being made to tag along. After driving five hours to Atlanta, they arrived early and took seats in the middle section of the well-known hotel conference room. The room wasn't that large and it was crowded.

She squirmed in her seat. "Be right back."

Leo looked at some of the name tags and the large companies represented. Melinda's warning whispered in the back of his mind. No way could his company compete against these guys. Sweat beaded his brow as he continued to watch the players swagger with confidence around the room and oily smiles as they greeted each other.

What was I thinking? Thompson picked the wrong guy, wrong company.

When the representative of a well-known Fortune 500 company squeezed past him to take a seat further in the row, Leo admitted he was out of his league. He stood and walked into the lobby filled with comfortable looking furnishings in heavy dark woods and geometrical patterns in nautical shades of blues, greens and beige. Large green leafy plants stood in every corner denying him a spot to wait for Barb in the shadows.

"What's wrong?" she asked when she saw him standing outside the meeting room.

"This isn't something we can do." When the words left his mouth, he recognized his mistake immediately and rushed to rephrase his comments. "I mean I don't want to do it." He prayed she'd just go along and not force him to admit he wasn't one hundred percent certain his decoy concept would work.

She stuffed her hands in the pockets of her leather jacket and looked up at him with surprise and pity. The look was so out of character for her he couldn't describe it. "You're scared?"

So they were going to do this. He took her elbow and moved to the other side of the hall. "I just don't think it's the right time to bid, that's all."

"Why?"

"The competition … they've been doing this a long time, we can't compete."

"Why not? You think they're better? They have more E&E's? A faster response rate? More decoys? Or ops?"

He stared into her eyes as her questions raked across his skin, serving as a wakeup call and bolstering his confidence. How many times had he told her and the decoys they had the top information team in the country? Too many to count. He'd allowed fear—yeah, he could admit it to himself—to run him out the room before hearing the details about the job.

"No. No one's better doing what we do."

She smiled. "We're already here so let's take it one step at a time. First, the job description, then listen to the questions, and last make a decision. Fair?"

Although he no longer needed her pep talks, he nodded, fully prepared to sit through to the end and realistically gauge if this was a job his company could do. No private company had a faster response rate or larger single network. Sometimes bigger equated to slower, and when you needed to track people on the move, fast worked better.

"Let's go inside."

They took seats at the back and for the next two hours listened as the speaker discussed the elements of the contract as if he read from a script. During the Q&A, he called many of the people in the audience by their first name. Leo questioned his ability to build such a large organization in the time allocated. When the last question was answered, the moderator dismissed the group.

Silent, Leo and Barb stood to leave.

"Leo."

He and Barb turned as a slender white guy with thinning brown hair and deep-set brown eyes moved in their direction. Several heads turned and watched as he stuck out his hand.

Leo accepted it.

"Barnaby Thompson, I'm the face behind the emails," he said in a lowered voice. "I told you about this conference." He glanced around the room and then at them. "You got time for lunch?"

"Yeah." Leo gauged by the attention they received this request wasn't normal.

"Barnaby, join me for lunch?" the guy who worked for the Fortune 500 company asked. His gaze flicked from Leo's name tag to Barb's.

"Sorry, Tim, I've got plans. Good to see you though." Thompson turned and ushered Leo and Barb through a side door and out the hotel through another exit.

"Sure, how long are you in town?" Tim asked, his face neutral as he stared at Thompson's back.

Barb looked at Leo. He shrugged.

"We can follow you," Leo said when Thompson headed toward a dark vehicle with its engine running.

"I'll bring you back here after lunch." Thompson opened the back door. Barb slid in first, then Leo, and Thompson entered last. The driver pulled out.

As Thompson's window slid up, Leo noticed several men looking at them with interest. Melinda's warning slammed into him. This was an entirely different league.

"Thanks for coming today, I wasn't sure you'd accept the RFP, but when your receptionist said you were out of the office I hoped you'd be here."

"Didn't hurt to hear more about it. Interesting work for sure," Leo said, his thoughts bouncing around the terms of the contract and the time frame.

"Good. Do you think you'll place a bid?" Thompson asked, watching him.

Leo's stomach clenched at the thought of the confrontation or headaches that seemed to accompany these jobs. "I don't know. When we get back to the office, we'll play around with the numbers, talk to a couple of subcontractors for the armed work, see what comes out of it."

Thompson handed him a large folder.

Leo opened and looked at the papers inside.

"That's the name of a software program that'll spit out a contract damn near perfect. There's also a sample of a contract so you get an idea of what's necessary." Thompson paused. "Your company has done several jobs for me and has another one in queue. As soon as Green arrives in town, I have no doubt that job will be completed efficiently and on time." He took a breath and looked at Leo. "No other contractor produces as quickly and thoroughly as you have. I want you to do more work for us, but we need to go through a few channels. I'll continue sending you assignments. If you can stay out of trouble and submit a good proposal, I assure you it'll be seriously considered."

Unable to immediately respond, Leo stared at Thompson for a few seconds and then nodded. "Thank you, we always do our best on any job sent our way, like I said, we'll play with the numbers—"

"The numbers don't matter, just submit a good proposal, one laid out with justifiable costs for what you provide. Use the cases you've done for me as examples, play up the turnaround time and the one hundred percent accuracy. Most importantly, because your company's new and you're young, stay out of trouble, no bad press. Keep the same low profile you've always had and everything should be fine."

"Thank you. We've stayed under radar so far," Leo said, squashing a memory of the collapse of a well known financial institution because of Venom.

"But you've never bid on a multimillion dollar contract before. I'm not going to lie, change is hard. However, if we don't change how we gather information to keep up with the times, we won't succeed. You hit something big that works, others aren't going to like it or you. The jobs I've given you were taken from other places, questions have been asked. The old boys are sniffing around."

"Because of a contract?" Barb asked in a disbelieving tone.

Thompson looked at her and smiled. "A multimillion dollar contract that can make or break a company's bottom line. This is no game for these guys. I'm telling you this so you understand and have a better picture of the offer. With this contract you can expand your operation to seven states over the course of seven years, maybe longer if necessary, with a consistent paycheck as long as you provide the services you already provide. Think about the benefits to your staff, you'll help more college students that's for sure. If they outweigh the cons in your mind, submit the proposal. I'd like more agencies to use your services."

As sales pitches went, Thompson's was awesome. The car stopped and they headed into the restaurant. One of the men from the conference stood outside and watched them approach. He flicked his cigarette onto the pavement after they passed and entered behind them.

Thompson told the hostess he wanted a table for three when the gentleman behind them spoke. "Mr. Thompson your party is waiting for you in the back."

Thompson frowned, glanced at the man from outside and spoke to the hostess. "A table for three please."

Her glance slid from Thompson to the man standing next to Barb. When he didn't say anything else, the hostess pulled the menus. "Follow me, please."

Thompson stepped aside so Barb could go first. Leo saw him glare at the silent man before following them to the table.

Once seated, Thompson offered Barb a smile and looked at his menu. During lunch they talked sports, colleges, and weather, everything except the RFP. Thirty minutes later as they finished their meal, the driver came in and whispered into Thompson's ear. A grimace flashed across his face and then he masked it.

"Seems my presence is required elsewhere," Thompson said as the driver walked off. "If you'll excuse me for a few minutes, I need to greet a few people and then take you back to your car." He wiped his mouth, stood, and pointed at Leo. "You can do this." He walked off.

Barb looked at him and whispered, "This is some serious shit. Did you see that dude outside?"

"Yeah." He didn't want to tell her he wasn't interested in submitting the proposal, not if they had to deal with all this, but as soon as they were alone in the car he'd let her know.

The driver returned to their table. "If you'll follow me, I'll drive you to your car."

The surprised expression on Barb's face probably mirrored his. Nevertheless, Leo stood, tossed fifty dollars on the table, and followed the driver.

When they reached the door, Thompson separated from a group of men and walked over to them. He shook Leo's hand and slapped his shoulder. "It was nice meeting you.

Maybe I'll let my son attend Duke after all. Thanks for catching up. Remember what I said." He winked and returned to the men he'd been talking with.

Leo and Barb walked out and slid into the back seat of the car. Neither spoke the short five minute drive to the hotel where the driver stopped in the front parking lot.

"Thank you," Leo said.

Barb waved at the driver as he pulled off. They walked toward Leo's silver S560 Mercedes in silence. Before they reached the car, but after he unlocked the doors with the remote, the man from the restaurant walked toward them. Leo did a double take as he realized the man must've followed them.

"Excuse me," he called out, his voice low and gritty, as he waved at them.

The ill-fitting charcoal gray suit sported wrinkles across the front as if it'd been rolled in a ball and shaken out just now. The cuffs in his pants dragged the ground and showed signs of wear. His spotless white shirt seemed out of place with everything else, and Leo couldn't drag his gaze from the contradiction. Leo waved Barb into the car. She ignored it and stood beside him.

"Yes?" Leo saw his face mirrored in the sunglasses lodged on the man's square face.

"You Leo Grit?"

"Yes. Who are you?" He clutched his cell phone in his right hand, relaxed a fraction, and triple tapped the screen to start recording.

"Word on the street is you're thinking about bidding on that government contract."

Leo stiffened and raised one brow. "Word on the street? What street?" His voice sounded strong, unaffected, he should've been an actor.

"Just a word of advice, son, don't do it. This isn't a game for little boys trying to prove they're men. Give yourself a few years, grow some chest hair, and then maybe you can play with the big boys."

"Who the fuck do you think you are?" Barb yelled.

The hairs on the back of Leo's neck rose as the comments and insults rolled across his mind. People didn't threaten people out in the open, not like this.

"Got the little butch bitch pretending to be a man, huh?" He chuckled. "This isn't for you. Go on, go home, don't waste your time on this. You'll never win."

Leo's vocal chords froze with disbelief. They stood outside a well-known hotel with people standing all around and this … this person had the audacity to tell him what to do as if he were a child. Heat rose fast and swiftly through him. His fist clenched and his nostrils flared as he stared down at the smug son of a bitch.

"Bastard," Barb snapped.

Leo held onto her arm as a sense of calm settled on his shoulder. He'd deal with this greasy bastard. "Who the fuck are you?" Leo asked in a slow, measured tone while pulling out his phone and snapping a picture.

"Your worst nightmare if you don't listen to my advice." He pulled his coat together and strode toward the valet, who held the door open for him. He tipped the guy and drove past Leo without another glance.

Chapter 8

Leo leaned back in his chair and stared out his office window. The wind picked up and rain was expected later tonight. He unclenched his jaw and exhaled. Butterflies flit about in his belly as he gazed at the trees separating his building from the houses on the other side. Had he made a mistake by submitting that bid? What were the chances he'd win? Thompson seemed to think he could do it, but those men in the restaurant seemed angry, concerned. Something he didn't ever want to be, not over a job. Had he allowed his pride to override common sense? Perhaps. But it was done.

Samuel Fuller. The man who threatened him. The man indirectly responsible for him submitting that bid was a former marine, employed as a security expert for an untraceable company. Divorced, one daughter, Amelia, in college. His former wife remarried the day after the divorce finalized during his deployment. Fuller earned several medals and received an honorable discharge. During his last overseas assignment, he'd been injured and spent two months in the hospital. Details regarding his physical condition were limited, but financially Fuller was set.

When Fuller verbally accosted him out of the blue, shock robbed Leo of speech. Afterward he thought of so many smart comebacks but planned to make his feelings known another way. It had been years since he'd worn his black hacker's cap, but for Fuller Leo made an exception. Tate Holdings showed up repeatedly in Fuller's bank records. Leo couldn't find a company with that name but would eventually. By the end of the week he'd know everything he could about the man who claimed to be a bad nightmare.

Guns? Not his thing. He preferred a different weapon. Fuller had no idea what he'd started or the real meaning of a nightmare.

Leo's phone vibrated. He looked at the caller ID.

"Jackson, how's it going?" he said in an upbeat note to disguise his unease over dealing with an unknown. Barb suggested they use Jackson's company as a subcontractor to handle the surveillance and armed security portions of the contract. Based on preliminary research, Jackson's company met the requirements, but Leo didn't know the guy, not in the way he needed to know a partner.

"Good, did you get those numbers and information from Cyndy?"

"Yes, it's included and submitted within the bid," Leo said.

"You're done already?" Jackson sounded surprised.

The software Thompson suggested streamlined the process by asking a lot of questions upfront and then filled in the blanks creating a customized, polished narrative. He'd been impressed.

"Yeah. I sent if off this morning. Glad to get that done, now I've got to clear my desk." He looked at his empty desk and returned his gaze to the window.

"I hear you. Just wanted to be sure you got everything you needed from me and to thank you for considering my firm. I appreciate that," Jackson said.

Mark, a decoy, worked for Jackson as well and had nothing but positive things to say about the man and the way he conducted business.

"Your reputation preceded you, and if we win the contract I'm sure it'll be a good deal for the both of us." They exchanged a brief round of thanks. Leo clicked off to study the pattern of tree placements outside while going over the particulars of the contract in his mind.

Boot heels clicked on the floor. He turned in the chair as Barb entered the room. She closed the door and grabbed the seat in front of his desk. Neither said anything for a few minutes.

Initially, Barb had been furious after the bid conference, ready to gut Fuller on the spot, but after she calmed down she wasn't sure they should go forward. The moment Fuller threatened him, forward became the only direction to go.

"Did you send it?"

"Yes." He'd told her he would yesterday.

"What if we lose everything?"

"That's a stretch isn't it? How can I lose everything by placing a bid I probably won't win?" The numbers he'd submitted were higher than the ones on past bids. Winning wasn't his real objective. In time he'd expand, but he'd do it at his own pace.

"You sure about this? What if that asshole comes after you?"

He shrugged, trying to display a calm he didn't feel. "What if he doesn't?"

She stared at him for a few seconds. "You spent a week and a half writing that thing, do you want to expand that bad?"

"No, not really, but no one's going to tell me I can't. Win or lose, I fight for my right to try." As far as he was concerned, she should understand ... or not.

She bit her nail and looked at his desk. "We have that decoy job tonight. Is it still on?"

He didn't understand what one had to do with the other. "Yes, Thompson sent instructions to do it tonight. Are Denise and Stacy ready?"

"Yeah." Barb exhaled. "We're all ready." She looked at him. "He was such an asshole."

He chuckled. "Yeah he was. Karma's a bitch."

Leo wondered if Tate Holdings was the company that hired Fuller to threaten them. He also had eyes and ears watching if Fuller came to town. They'd give him a nice North Carolina welcome.

"We have some new equipment Craig worked on. Stop by and pick it up before he heads out," Leo said.

She stood and headed toward the door. "You've got the board?"

"Yeah." He didn't add that he always worked the board for this client. If anything went wrong, he'd rather be the one standing in front of the bull's-eye.

"Good and good luck on the contract," she said.

"You don't mean that, but I love you anyway," he said smiling to pull her out of her funk. The last thing they needed was to fold beneath fear and intimidation.

Barb stopped at the door. "How's Melinda doing?"

The day after they returned from the bid conference in Atlanta, Melinda popped into the office, voicing her concern over their discussion about Fuller's threats. Barb had been in his office, pulling data for him at the time, and heard Melinda before she realized he wasn't alone.

"Good." He didn't discuss his private life, not that he was sure he and Melinda had a private life yet. She seemed interested in him and was good company. He hoped something would work out. Like Derrick and his lady, Leo would love to spend a weekend with the sexy attorney in the mountains or anywhere, preferably sooner than later.

Barb smiled and left.

Leo returned to his view to the window. Thunder rumbled in the distance. The skies darkened as the clouds released their bounty. Rain splattered against the window pane.

"If I were superstitious, this would be an omen," he murmured and rubbed his stomach to ease the tension

Chapter 9

Soft music played in the background of the hotel bar. Wall-to-wall windows showcased glistening sidewalks from the earlier downpour. Irregular snatches of conversation and occasional outbursts of laughter added to the moderate upbeat atmosphere in the space. Rainy weather kept the locals away. There was plenty of room around the bar to sit, grab a quick bite, and make friends.

"I'm not interested in married men, sorry." Stacy turned away from Noel Green with just the right amount of disdain and continued her conversation with Denise. Both women, young, bright-eyed, and beautiful, sat at the bar sipping drinks and talking softly.

Noel stared at Stacy's back for a few moments, threw back his cocktail, and leaned forward on the gleaming wood bar.

Sitting two seats from Green but across from Stacy, Barb stared into her beer with her head down and phone turned toward Noel, taking pictures. Stacy had read Green like a well-used book and played her role to perfection.

Their client wanted Green to remain in the bar for the next thirty minutes to an hour and hired decoys to keep him entertained. When the older man with thinning brown hair and an over-sized belly to match his ego entered the hotel bar, his gaze zeroed in on the young college students. He almost tripped over his feet to sit near them. Whoever filled out the paperwork for this job knew exactly what carrot to put in front of Green.

Barb looked at Greg, the bartender, and nodded.

He headed to Noel. "Can I get you another drink, sir?"

"Yes, and whatever the lady and her friend want as well." Green pointed to Stacy and Denise.

Stacy glanced at him over her shoulder and smiled. "Thank you."

Green's entire face reddened and then softened as he stared at the young woman who could be his granddaughter. He withdrew a credit card, looked at it for a second, and then pulled out another one. He handed it to Greg.

"I'll need to see some ID, sir." Greg stared at the card for a few seconds and then met Green's stare.

"What? What you *men*? I meant, mean," Green said in a brusque tone.

Barb checked her notes to see how many drinks he'd had. Three? And he stumbled over his words already?

"Identification for the credit card, sir." Greg's tone was firm and respectful.

Green showed him his driver's license.

"Thank you, Mr. Green and welcome to Greensboro, North Carolina," Greg said, his voice loud enough that it'd be picked up on Stacy's recording of her conversation with the man.

Now that the target was positively identified with proof of his whereabouts, Barb sent pictures to Leo at the office.

The place smelled of fresh-ground roasted coffee, Italian spices, and freshly baked bread. If the job was longer, she'd order more than a soft drink. Her stomach growled as she noticed the few patrons seated at tables enjoying their meals. She grabbed a handful of peanuts and looked around the bar area, noting the exits and people, then back at Stacy. Their glances brushed and she nodded.

Stacy fiddled with her necklace, engaging the recorder. Denise turned aside and did the same.

"Clients been alerted the target's in the bar. We are live," Leo said.

Stacy and Green chatted off and on for the next twenty minutes. Whenever he got quiet, she'd turn and ignore him, which spurred him to ask her more questions.

Barb placed her hand on her stomach. She'd been queasy since they left Atlanta and the damn bid conference. Why did she talk Leo into going? He hadn't really been interested, but no, she went on and on about expanding, buying new equipment, the whole damn enchilada. When would she learn to keep her mouth shut? Now Leo—who didn't do violence, didn't even own a gun, and probably couldn't kick his own ass—could be in the fight of his life, trying to prove something. Maybe she needed to start carrying her pistol just in case that assshole showed up at the office.

"Barb?" Leo said.

She turned away from the target and placed her phone next to her ear to give the illusion she was speaking to someone.

"I just got the all clear. Wrap it up, fill out those reports, and call it a night," Leo said.

"On it." She glanced at her watch. They'd been at the bar an hour. She kept the phone to her ear, looked at Denise, and gave her the signal.

"I'm not married," Green said, his words slurring a bit.

"I am," Stacy said and held up her hand, showing a wedding band she'd slipped on.

Green wore a puzzled expression and then glowered. Barb looked at him, prepared to step in, when Denise turned and looked at the man.

"You dropped your wallet." She pointed to the floor.

He pushed back and almost fell while looking down at the ground. "How'd it get out my pocket?" Staggering, he

pointed a finger at Denise who sat on the opposite side of
Stacy, a good distance from him.

"You tried to steal it?!" His voice rose at the end.

Barb noticed the surprise and the dark look on her
operatives' faces. Seniors, majoring in pre-law, meant
nothing beneath the hateful accusation from this drunken lout.
Their training should encourage them to ignore him and leave
gracefully. Barb waited to see if she'd been successful
training these two.

"Sir, is there a problem?" Greg asked, his voice terse.

Green pointed at Denise. "Her, the black one ... she tried
to take my wallet and threw it on the floor."

Denise's jaw tightened as she stood.

"Easy," Leo said in their earphones. "He's drunk. Time
to leave, ladies."

Stacy jumped in front of Denise. "You racist asshole.
We should press charges against you for masquerading as a
damn human being! Clearly you haven't evolved and need to
get your drunk ass out of here before it gets kicked." She
turned to Denise. "What he'd prefer is for his wallet to stay
on the floor so somebody else can find it. Then he'll blame
someone else for his sorry situation." She bent, picked it up,
and threw it on the counter. "You ungrateful asshole. Come
on, Nee. We don't need to breathe the same air as this piece
of garbage." She took the drink he'd bought her and poured it
in his half empty glass of beer.

"I don't want a damn thing from rednecks." Stacy
grabbed her bag with one hand and Denise's arm with the
other and they marched out the door.

Heads turned as they passed but the ladies never looked
back. The manager pulled Greg to the side, whispering, and
then walked off.

Green stood staring at the spot where Stacy had stood
and then looked at Greg. "Now that's a woman. Wish my

wife had half of her fire." He returned to his seat at the bar and grabbed his glass.

Behind the man, Barb rolled her eyes. She'd need to work with Stacy on her dramatic flair. They weren't in a courtroom, but she'd done her job. Barb waited around a few minutes to make sure Green didn't try and follow the ladies before leaving to meet them back at the office.

She signed the check and returned it to Greg. "Thanks, everything was excellent as usual."

Greg looked at the paper and smiled, no doubt pleased with the large tip. "Thank you. Come back again."

Green glanced at her, frowned, and finished off his glass. Accustomed to male reaction to her short buzz cut, black tee, jeans and boots, she ignored him and waited for Leo to say the ladies were on their way in.

"The babies are in the car on their way to the office," Leo said.

"On my way." She stood. "Have a good evening," she told Greg.

"You too," Greg said.

"Is that a dyke?" Green asked, not bothering to lower his voice.

Barb whirled around. "Why yes. Yes I am."

Green's mouth dropped open and then he scowled as she laughed and walked out.

Chapter 10

"Where are we on this contract?" Andy Wagram sitting at his desk asked curious how Fuller would respond.

"It's been submitted. Oversight's reviewing all the bids," Fuller said.

Wagram's gaze narrowed. "Why the hell are they doing that? We've held this contract for four cycles. Hell, we just convinced the old windbags to lengthen the contract from three years to seven." He raised his hands, palms up to change the question. "What's different this time?"

Fuller leaned back in his chair. "Thompson's been giving jobs to some kid in North Carolina. Somehow convinced him to place a bid and is putting pressure on the committee to follow procedures."

"Procedures? Now they're following procedures?" Wagram's voice rose, along with his arms. He dropped them while shaking his head. "Perhaps they need to be reminded how this process works. We submit a bid, they accept. That's the way everyone agreed this would go, damned if they renege now. Not happening." He slammed his palm on the table. The empty cup bounced and rolled on to the floor.

Of all the times for the procurement committee to grow balls. Each member in the consortium took turns submitting the RFP for the group so that it appeared the procurement team used different companies. He'd pulled the short straw this time and couldn't afford to lose. They'd replace him in the organization—one of the rules *he'd* insisted on when they formed the consortium. His company couldn't afford the loss of business. He'd borrowed heavily for equipment to meet the criteria of the new contract, to default would shut him down.

His wife's family, the Tates, wouldn't hesitate one moment to fling this failure in his face. Hell, no telling what his wife would do if he couldn't maintain the several homes they owned. Chances are she'd side with her family against him again. No loyalty there.

The sweetest face rose in his vision, Loren, his soulmate and lover housed in an exclusive section of southwest Albuquerque. The thought of life without her chilled his soul.

"We cannot lose that contract." He stared at Fuller.

Several years ago they'd met when Fuller returned from his last deployment and attended a bid conference as security. Wagram read the anger and greed in the man's eyes and took him to lunch. A bargain had been struck that day. He paid Fuller through his wife's family company. Fuller's job expanded from keeping him abreast of any jobs his company might be interested in to extra muscle when needed and anything in between.

Fuller cracked his knuckle and met Wagram's gaze. "I did warn him not to submit the bid. That was the least I could do."

Wagram leaned back and watched the cynical smile form on Fuller's face. Times like these he wondered if Fuller had lost touch with humanity. The man had a cruel streak that scared Wagram.

"You cannot kill or hurt him physically, because no matter what we say, it'll reflect badly on this group. Smothers and Gates would have heart failures if anything dirty touched their names."

Fuller glanced at him, his tone sarcastic. "Aww, you're no fun."

Wagram waved away his comment. "Who is this guy?"

Fuller pulled out a small tablet and touched the screen a few times. "Computer geek extraordinaire. Won lots of contests in high school and college. Can't be one hundred percent sure, but I think he created whatever software he's using during college. Graduated with an MBA and masters in Computer Science." He looked at Wagram. "Check this out. His thesis centered on using a large network of people to upload stuff using their cell phones, and somehow he uses it to find people or catch people in criminal acts." Fuller scratched his head while looking at his device.

"Really? How'd he prove it?" Intrigued Wagram sat forward.

"Used students from four campuses as test subjects, received high marks. A year later his company started. Been open a total of three years, even though the company's been on the books for five." He looked at Wagram.

"Thompson uses him?"

"Yes. From what I've found out, this software catalogs information from cell phones that helps his clients gather whatever Intel they need," Fuller said in a mocking tone.

Wagram stared at him. "You don't believe it works?" The idea fascinated him. If this worked, it could increase response times dramatically. He understood the appeal.

"He uses college students and untrained civilians. Need I say more?"

Fuller was one of those vets who believed the military had a lock down on particular skillsets and snubbed anyone who hadn't been trained through certain channels.

"Yet, Thompson uses him in North Carolina where Jackson has an office. Why not use Jackson?" Wagram asked.

Fuller's jaw clenched. He didn't respond. Wagram knew he'd hit a sore spot mentioning Fuller's rival.

"I'll have someone look into the whole concept, see how viable it is, if it can be reproduced. If it's good enough for that tightwad, tight-laced Thompson to use, it's something the consortium needs to be aware of. Perhaps we can add it to our list of services in the future." He looked at Fuller, who stared at his tablet.

"In the meantime how do we stop this computer asshole from stealing our contract?"

Fuller slowly turned to meet his gaze. "If I can't touch him physically, we go after his company. Make it a nonviable competitor."

"Sounds good. Do it."

Wagram wondered what Fuller planned to do but didn't ask, better to not know. Instead, he'd have his contact reach out to several hackers to get their take on the concept. If the programming could be penetrated, it could be stolen and copied. That appealed to him on several levels.

Chapter 11

Later that week, Barb walked into Leo's office, closed the door, and took a seat in the chair. "Someone has an ad for decoys in the paper. They're paying a dollar more an hour than us and get this, promising minimum pay whether they work or not. I've had three calls from our decoys this morning asking if this was our company since the initials of that new company are the same - GI."

Leo's fingers stopped moving across the keyboard, and he turned from the report he'd been writing. "Really? That's ... that's weird."

"Yeah, here's the clincher: to work for that company, to get the solid weekly guarantee, you can't work for anyone else in the same kind of work."

Leo stared at her and leaned back in his chair. "Our E&Es sign non-disclosure agreements when hired instead of a non-compete. My attorney believed restricting employees from sharing the app and company information was sufficient. Maybe I need to rethink this."

Barb didn't say anything.

"Thoughts?"

She tilted her head to the side and pursed her lips. "You know what I think? It's those bastards who don't want you to win the bid. When will they announce the winner anyway?"

"Two weeks. Thompson said it's on a fast track or something." Leo hadn't paid much attention at the time because he hadn't planned on submitting.

"Two weeks and then this is over, or does it really begin? How long will they pay people to not work for us?" She paused and leaned back in the chair. A slow smile climbed her face. "That's a serious payout. It could run into the millions if they take on a lot of people."

"Maybe they've created software and plan to compete, who knows. We can't get bogged down by what they're doing. Stay focused on what we've always done, provide top service for our clients." He spoke the words without believing them, but he needed time to think and investigate the matter.

"You're right. Hey, maybe I'll send an email to all the people we didn't hire and tell them to sign up with this company. Stretch their budget." She stood up smiling. "What they'll do is string everybody along and never pay anything. Plus, I doubt anyone we've ever used will drop us without seeing some money from the other camp anyway. Students are too smart to put their eggs in one basket."

Leo hoped Barb's optimism was true. "Don't borrow trouble."

"Right, borrowing is not the word I'd use."

When she left he returned to the report, but his thoughts lingered on this new problem. He stopped typing and stared at the keyboard for a few seconds. Were they trying to confuse people? Muddy the waters so people would think this new company was his? He opened another screen and completed a search. It didn't take long to find the ad.

Wanted. People with cell phones who can upload videos and pictures to our website. Guaranteed part-time pay. Submit application to our website.

On their website they promised one hundred dollars per week guarantee, statewide non-disclosure and non-compete for eighteen months.

Leo called Melinda and told her about the ad. "Can I fight this?"

"Let me get back to you on this," she said. "I'm on my way to court."

He clicked off. Most students he hired would only see the one hundred dollars a week and not care about the rest.

Leo wrote a detailed memo breaking down the competitor's job offer and explaining the terminology. He ended it saying he'd respect their choice and wished them the best. He sent the message to everyone in his network.

Ten minutes later Barb returned to his office smiling. "Well done. Very classy. You handled that like a pro. Whoever we lose after that message, good riddance. I opened the forum so they could discuss the matter online, so far the comments are real positive on our behalf."

"Great. It's expensive hiring and training decoys. I'd hate to lose them." He thought of Griff, Tag, Derrick, Craig, Denise, and Stacy specifically.

"I never thought we'd lose a large number, but you never know." She laughed.

Curious, he looked at her. "What did you do?"

"I sent a message to the people we never hired, the ones who didn't pass the drug or background tests. I thought they should know about the wonderful opportunity offered by another company. Even told them they'd have to sign a non-compete, taking them off our radar for a while." She sighed dramatically. "Just trying to help, you know."

Leo smiled.

Barb grinned. "Hey, if they've got that big a budget to pay people, they'll have thousands of applications. You were right. We can't focus on their bullshit. We've got work to do."

He nodded, glad to see her in better spirits.

"That surveillance job for the insurance company … Griff worked it last night. The target stays in his hotel most of the day and goes to a strip club at night. Tag and Derrick can't follow him inside but can wait in the parking lot if that'll work," she said.

College students weren't welcomed in the nicer strip clubs because they were horrible tippers. La Fortuna, where the target chose to spend the bulk of his evenings, was one of those.

"Griff already placed a tracker on the target's car, so that'll help. Make sure everyone has the right frequency so they can stay far enough behind this guy. See if Derrick can work the 1:00 pm – 8:00 pm shift. Give Tag four in the morning to noon since his classes are later in the day. That way Griff works 8:00 pm till 4:00 am and can follow the target into the club. If Derrick can't work that shift, put Craig on it during the week and Derrick on the weekend."

She nodded while tapping her tablet.

"Also I've activated the E&Es at the front desk of that hotel and the maids to take pictures of the target anytime they see him. Unfortunately, the maid doesn't work his floor but she said she'd try to get reassigned there soon."

"Sounds good. Did Cherise tell you Mrs. Carter has left a ton of messages on the phone we assigned Stacy? Sent her some emails too."

"Yeah, they're in the files. I haven't heard from Mr. Carter since he received my report. He wasn't happy."

She snorted. "Don't be fooled. Lots of men enjoy seeing their wives with other people. Mrs. Carter's been doing this a long time. Not sure how long she's paid for it, but she's been with women before."

"I can't imagine sharing the little time I have now and then to split that with someone else?" He shook his head, his thoughts traveling to Melinda. They'd talked back and forth on the phone and set up another dinner date for later this week.

"Me neither. That's why I'm taking it slow with Rebekkah."

He looked up at her. "Who? Haven't heard that name before."

"We met that night at Lingerie and have gone out a few times. She's nice, but we'll see."

Like him, Barb was private regarding her social life. It surprised him she volunteered any information.

Leo nodded. "Good plan, no rush if it's right. Right?"

She winked. "Riiiight. What else do we have?"

"Nothing else. Thompson sent a notice he has another one coming soon, but it's not here yet."

"Awesome. It'd be nice to go home early for a change."

Leo glanced out the window. "Yeah, nice."

His phone beeped. *Melinda.* "Hi, you still in court?" he asked.

"No, the doctor didn't show up. I asked for a continuance. You want to get together later for dinner? My treat this time. We can talk about non-competes."

"Sounds good, but my treat. What do you have a taste for?" He ran his hands through his hair and glanced at the clock on his desk. Plenty of time to go home, shower, and dress before picking her up from her place.

"Seafood. I've been craving shrimp since I saw a commercial on TV."

"Give me your address. I'll pick you up." He waited to see how she responded to his moving this into a date column.

She cleared her throat and rattled off her address. "I need to finish a few things here before going home. Can we leave in a couple hours?" Her voice sounded uncertain. He couldn't imagine she'd think he wouldn't wait two hours or more to spend time with her.

"That works for me. Pick you up at seven-thirty."

Pleased with the plans he'd made for the night, he walked up front to make sure Cherise completed payroll and Craig had finished working on the mini-microphones. Five guys whose ages could range anywhere from sixteen to twenty-five, loaded with tattoos and wearing sagging pants and tee shirts walked into the lobby as he turned the corner.

Interesting.

"Is this where we get jobs using our phones," a guy asked.

"We're not hiring right now," Leo said, watching the guys carefully while fingering his phone.

"I called the phone number on the website. It gave this address to come and fill out applications," the guy said, looking around.

The determined looks from these guys changed the game from frivolous copycat to serious trouble. Seems he'd need to employ Jackson's services now rather than later. "One second. Let me see what I can do." He sent Jackson a text, giving a brief outline, and hired him right then. Jackson asked him to stall the guys for five to ten minutes until he and his men arrived.

Leo started recording.

"Seems there was a mix up. We'll take care of that in a few minutes. Jackson's looking for new hires." He tilted his head and then stuck out his free hand. "My name's Leo."

"Paco," the guy said bumping the back of his hand. None of the others spoke or bumped fists.

"You are talking about the job where you use your cell phone to take pictures and videos right?" Leo asked.

"Yeah, that's right."

"And you're paid two hundred bucks a week?"

"Two hundred? Dude said one hundred," another guy said. They looked at each other and then back at him.

"Call him again. I'm sure he'd pay two hundred a week."

Paco pulled out his phone and placed a called. A few seconds later he frowned and placed his phone in his pocket. "No answer. You know this dude?"

"Who?" Leo asked.

"The one using this place and hiring people. If he's paying some people two hundred and others one hundred … that shit ain't right."

Leo frowned. "Did you meet him? Can you describe him?"

"No, just called that number. He's on his way?"

"Jackson is on his way. He's looking to hire people."

"For two hundred a week?" Paco asked.

"Or more depending on what you do." Leo glanced at his watch and hoped Jackson would arrive soon. He didn't want any of his staff to hear this weird conversation. The whirring of the elevator delayed further talk.

Jackson and three guys strode toward him. One guy remained by the elevator. Another walked inside and turned right toward the conference room. Jackson and the third guy stopped next to Leo and offered him their hands.

"Good to see you, Jackson." Leo looked up at the former ranger who stood a good three inches over Leo's six feet. Whereas Leo would say his was an average build, there was nothing average about Jackson. Muscular from head to toe, he looked like a linebacker in jeans and a polo shirt with shoulder length blondish hair.

"Good to be here." Jackson turned and looked at the young men who stared at him with a question in their eyes. "You fella's looking for work?"

Paco frowned and held up his phone. "The ad said all we had to do was take pictures and upload them to this website. The number on the website said to come here to fill out paperwork."

Jackson frowned. "I have an ad to hire security workers. Using your phones are a part of it, but not the bulk of it." He looked at Leo and then back to the young guys. "On my website you can fill out an application and I'll call you if I'm interested." He scratched his head. "Sounds like somebody's playing games."

"Fucking right. I smelled shit when I saw it. Who'd pay when people put shit from their phones online all the time free? This was a waste of time. You shoulda told us that when we arrived." Paco glared at Leo, turned, and they all filed out.

"That sounded scripted," Leo said as he and Jackson walked to his office and watched the exterior security cameras. Paco, surrounded by the others, was on the phone looking back at the office, pointing and nodding.

"They'll be back. Probably tonight or one night this week," Jackson said, looking at him.

Leo rubbed the back of his neck while watching the five men enter a silver SUV. He'd pull the plates in a few minutes, but he needed a few seconds to process his office building had just been targeted for vandalism and possibly more.

"What do I do?" he asked as soon as the tight band around his chest loosened.

"This is Timms." He pointed to the man who'd stood quietly in the background. "He'll head up your security team. I should've thought of this when you explained the job. It's not uncommon."

"What?" Leo's head jerked up.

Jackson snorted. "Money brings out the worst in men. A lot of money could start a war."

Leo wished he'd never listened to Thompson or submitted that damn bid.

"As I was saying, Timms will head up the team here. Plus, I'll let a friend of mine, Detective Bronson with the police department, know what happened."

"Thanks."

"The greatest need for security will be at night. Five men will be available, two on the grounds and three inside initially. During the day, one security officer will monitor access to this floor and maybe another person as backup. If that asshole is naming this address for applications, you're going to need to counter that in some way."

Jackson's calm, methodical approach tamped down Leo's rising fear, allowing him to think clearer. Things were being handled.

"I can place an ad stating it's not me, call them out for fraud."

"If that information is being given on a phone, the recording can easily be changed and that leaves you in a predicament. Why not just have a couple signs printed and have them placed downstairs saying a mistake was made? That way the other company looks like the bad guy, not you.
"

"What if we take a copy of the recording? Press charges?" Leo asked, it would be better to avoid problems if possible.

"Sure, contact your attorney, explain what's going on, shouldn't be too hard to get the paper to remove the ad after that. Especially if there's been no contact on your part."

Leo remembered Barb had sent emails to the people they hadn't hired. What if someone told the copycat company and this was their way of fighting back. Damn. He needed to talk to Melinda about this.

"You're right, makes sense." Leo paused and leaned against his desk. "Can I stop this? If I withdraw my bid, I mean?"

Jackson's face blanked.

Leo sensed he'd made a terrible mistake, but he didn't want his people hurt over a bid he didn't think he'd win.

"I don't know. Ask your contact, see what he says." Jackson paused. "You had no idea what you were getting into by submitting that contract did you?"

Leo drew in a breath and then released it. "I didn't believe this could happen is the better way to say it. I can't believe everyone in that room is being attacked like this. It doesn't make any sense."

Jackson waved Timms out the room and took a seat. "You were singled out by a heavy player. He could've spared you all of this by ignoring you. Instead, his attention meant you are a possible contender for the job, whereas the others aren't. Companies hire people all the time to attend those conferences to watch to see who attends and if anything special happens."

"When I first walked into the room and saw the names of the companies bidding for that contract I knew I was in over my head." Could a Fortune 500 company be behind this? It was hard to believe. He looked at Jackson. "Who's doing this?"

"This person or persons is working for someone in line for this contract. Believe me when I tell you the guy or woman, attacking your company, making things difficult for you … this isn't personal. It's a job. Nothing more. They will do everything within their power to make this company look worse than a mom-and-pop operation on a dirt road in the country before that contract's awarded."

Leo ran his hand through his hair as the tight band squeezed his chest again. He'd started this. At the time he believed it was the right decision. He replayed Fuller's mocking comments after the conference in his mind and straightened his spine. Strings of code snaked through his mind. Lately, he'd been looking at some of his old programs and ventured into a couple underground rooms to hear the latest news.

"When this is over, I doubt anything will ever be the same around here." He wouldn't be the same, that's for sure.

Jackson's slow forming smile reached his eyes. "Glad I wasn't wrong about you."

Leo frowned.

"You're tough."

"No, I'm scared shitless for my business, my employees." *Going to jail if my secret gets out.*

"I can respect that. But you're not quitting. Takes strength to remain strong through your fear. Sensed that about you the first time we talked. It's the only reason I agreed to submit my company's name on your contract." Jackson stood and extended his hand.

Leo accepted it even as he rehashed Jackson's comments.

"My team will keep the physical part of your company secure. I'll have someone watching your house all day." He held up his hand to stop Leo's protest. "This isn't a game. What's happening now is annoying appetizers leading to a harsher main course. You're the head. Cut off the head and what's left?"

Leo swallowed hard, unable to answer. An overwhelming desire to stroke his neck swept over him, but he kept his hand to the side.

"Twenty-four hour security on your house and a driver to take you back and forth each day until the contract's awarded."

Leo calculated the cost in his head and couldn't fathom how he'd pay for all of this and run the business. Wetting his lips, he raised a finger as if in school and asking permission to talk. When he realized his action, he put his hand down.

"Cost. What's this type of security going to cost me?"

Jackson looked down at him for a few minutes. "The cost of the men, nothing for the company, but you'll have to pay their wages." He said a ball park number and Leo relaxed. He could handle that without going in the red.

"Thanks. Here's what we can do," Leo said. "While your men are here, if you are on a job and need eyes and ears, my network is available for your use. The fees for my people is less than yours so that could help offset some of your administrative costs. Would that work?"

Jackson's eyes lit. "We'd barter or exchange services?"

"Yes. I need security which will pull your resources for a while. So we'll use mine to help make up the difference on some of your cases."

"That'll work. I appreciate it. Would it be possible to have Cyndy come over and meet with Cherise and get an understanding of billing and anything we need to know?"

"Yes. Cherise may be gone for the day, but I'll leave her a message that your office will get in contact with her."

Jackson headed to the door, looked back at Leo, and nodded. "I was right about you."

Chapter 12

"They were in your parking lot?" Melinda asked later that night at dinner.

Leo took a sip of water to cool the residual irritation running through him. "Yeah," he said and met her worried gaze across the table. "An hour after those five guys left, I got a call from security that twenty people arrived downstairs for training. Some claimed they had already done jobs for me and had gotten paid."

"Had they?"

"I don't know. What I do know is we had over 589 people signed up with our company and 59 cancelled their contracts today. I'm assuming to work for this new company." He took another sip.

"What did security do?" She broke the breadstick in half and took a bite.

"Handed out flyers that explained our position, that we did not authorize the company on the internet to use our name or address and had no idea who that company was."

Armed with the evidence of fraud, Leo made his case to the newspaper and they removed the ad. Barb contacted the college paper and all the news outlets in their target area explaining someone had played a hoax on the company.

"One of the reporters called and asked Barb a few questions which she referred to me," he said.

"Oh?"

"Yeah, I answered a few questions."

She frowned.

"What? I shouldn't have done that?" He leaned back as the waiter placed their salads on the table.

"Depends on the reporter, the paper, and what you said. If the paper doesn't care about the truth and wants to sensationalize the news to sell papers..." she tilted her head to the side and met his gaze "...then anything you say will be twisted to do that, sell papers. If they report news, then they may investigate it some and report the facts as they find them. Few news outlets simply repeat what you've said."

"Small paper in Charlotte she said. I'll ask Barb the name of it." The possible ramifications of more bad press weighed on him. So far they hadn't lost any clients and needed to be careful.

She nodded. "Do you want me to look into this? If a company is sending people to your office with job expectations with the intent to impact your business, you have recourse in the courts. I'll file an emergency injunction against that company to have the website removed until things are sorted."

"Yes, do that. How soon can that be done?" Hope filled his chest at the prospect of fixing this problem. Maybe he wouldn't need the additional security.

She smiled. "Can I finish dinner first?"

His face heated and he smiled. "Well, I guess so."

Melinda chuckled.

"Why don't I put you on retainer, that way you can handle things as they come up in the next two weeks."

"Two weeks?"

Leo nodded and then wiped his mouth with his napkin. "According to Jackson, the guy who owns the security company, this is common and should be over once the bid is decided."

"Hmm." She ate another piece of bread and then looked at him. "Well in that case, you're right about the retainer. I hate this is happening to you."

Thankful she didn't say I told you so, he nodded. "We'll get through it."

"How are your clients handling this?"

"No problems so far."

She nodded. "Good. Let me know if that changes because of this. We'll also sue for damages."

Leo stilled in his seat and stared at her as a well of gratitude rose and covered him. When he could speak, he swallowed. "Thank you, I appreciate it." Wisps of their former conversation when she asked him about being a father, having a family echoed in his ears.

Melinda's fork paused midway to her mouth as their gazes locked. "You're welcome. I've got you on this."

Unaccustomed to sharing the administrative burdens of his company, Jackson earlier and now Melinda, he didn't know what to say and nodded in appreciation of her support.

"Hello. Melinda," Dr. Wittier said as he passed their table.

"Hello," she said to the doctor's back. He sat alone at a table on the other side of the room. "He spoke to me as if he hadn't stood me up in court today." She looked over her shoulder at Wittier. "I wonder if he still goes to the warehouse."

Leo glanced at the doctor and shrugged. "Maybe." His tone reflected his 'who cares?' feeling about the doctor's personal life.

She leaned closer. "He's got to be the worse client ever, rarely shows up for his appointments, refuses to sign papers in a timely manner, and won't answer most of my questions. And he treated all of his attorneys that way, so it's not just me."

"It's not personal then." Leo took another bite.

Melinda glanced at the doctor again and then looked at him. "No, it's not. Excuse, me." She patted her lips with the cloth napkin, pushed back, and walked to the doctor's table. Leo half watched Melinda smile and talk to the doctor while thinking of the female who claimed to have sent information to his company yesterday.

That had been a lie. One he didn't challenge in front of the group of people reading the flyers or asking questions, but he recognized the potential problem if people uploaded pictures or videos with the expectation of payment. If the rogue company ordered the information, and didn't pay, that opened a different can of worms.

"Bingo. That simple conversation did more than months of appointments. He's coming in tomorrow to sign some papers and to discuss a legal matter I'd been trying to get him to deal with for a while." She gave him a thumbs-up.

Smiling, Leo returned the gesture. The rest of their meal passed in a comfortable, thoughtful silence. He liked that about her. After taking care of the tip, they walked outside. Timms pulled up and they slid in the backseat.

"Stop by the office before we take Ms. Union home. I want to check on things." Leo looked at Melinda. "I want to show you something."

"Okay," Timms said and pulled out.

She nodded and leaned against him. Leo took her hand and kissed the back of it. When this mess cleared, he'd like to spend some quality time with her.

The parking lot had emptied leaving the building with an abandoned appearance that didn't bother him at all. Leo ushered her into the console room and had her take a seat while he entered several passwords to access his system. The screen went from opaque to clear. He zoomed out and hundreds of blue dots and a red one filled the screen.

She leaned forward, her gaze roaming over the screen. "This is some sort of map. I recognize some of the street names." She pointed. "My office is near there."

"I don't have human children, but this is my baby, Ghost. The heart of my company. Every blue dot represents a person who signed up with my company as eyes and ears, or E&Es. That's all they do, allow me to see and record what they see wherever they are at a given time. I pay them for their time weekly through automatic draft. If a person can't or doesn't have a bank account, they can't work for me. If they don't pass a background and drug test, they can't work for me. We don't advertise in local papers. Never have. Several colleges allow us to post jobs in their papers or on job boards, but most of our employees are through referrals."

"This is amazing." She moved closer to the monitor and watched dots move. "Is this automatic? Do they keep their phones turned on or something?"

Leo smiled. "Not really. I created an app that's installed on their phones, it only sends images or video, not text, and only when I approve the transmission. The app connects their phones to the system, the system checks for steganography and other bugs just in case a decoy sends a virus in a coded image."

She stared at the board a few moments longer. "Images and videos only. Makes it almost impossible to breach. This is ... this is cutting edge. I can see how you're able to track a person fast. Why so many monitors?"

"To see and record different viewpoints from different decoys. If a target is at the mall or in a club, I may have three or five pairs of eyes recording. Those are saved, combined, and sent to the client."

Nodding, she stared as he zoomed into the area near her home. "Wow, you've got people everywhere."

"Everyone has a cell phone," Leo explained. "The people I hire receive minimal online training as E&Es. They receive a password which is only good for forty-eight hours to access the instruction module. If they don't finish or pass training and sign the confidentiality agreement, their application never hits the system."

"What's that red dot?"

"Staff specifically trained in decoy and surveillance work here in the office. When they aren't working, their lights are blue." He pointed to Griff's lone red light on the insurance surveillance job.

"This ... this is what scares them. They can't compete with this," she said with awe in her voice as she looked at him. "You created this? Own this?"

"Yeah. Built the software program, the hardware that houses everything, and the app." He placed his finger beneath her chin and closed her mouth.

Laughing, she pushed his hand away. "You've been busy. I cannot imagine the hours it took to build something like this."

"Building the program and hardware wasn't too bad. Protecting it ... that's ... that's the challenge." *Especially since he started his junior year of college.*

"How?" She pointed to the screen.

He smiled. "I've got certain things in place that keeps Ghost safe so far. Some things in the office are connected to the internet on a completely different server. This baby lives several secure places." Most of the money from the trust his grandparents left him went into building this place and the secure room to house his servers. If those were compromised, backup servers immediately went live and alerted him. No one had access to the keyless server room in his office. Zeke once called him paranoid; he preferred to think of it as careful.

"I'm not surprised. So whoever is playing copycat, how far do they go? Is there anything that I would see and know immediately if's not from you?"

Leo thought about it for a minute and then snapped his fingers. "I can show you if you allow me to download the app on your phone. You won't be active unless you went through the online training, and it won't hurt anything." He watched excitement blaze in her eyes as she dug out her phone and handed it to him.

Leo typed in a series of codes before connecting her phone to the system. He returned it to her.

"What's DU?"

He smiled. "Decoys United. Decoy University. Decoys Unlimited. I couldn't decide and picked those initials so I can use them all. Notice my logo or company initials are not on my app. That's the first thing. Second, if you accepted everything, went through the training, the app integrates with your phone on a base level and DU disappears. No one would ever know you worked here unless they traced the money. From the moment employment is accepted, Ghost gives the decoy a number." He clicked on several dots. "So even if a person somehow breached my system to this point, decoys are protected. The lives of the people I hire aren't disrupted by working here. I don't need people who want to be seen. They don't make good decoys."

Leo watched as she stared open mouthed at the monitor and shook her head.

"Amazing. I didn't understand why they asked you to bid, but I get it now. This is … unbelievably awesome."

His lungs expanded to the fullest and then he released air slowly, straightening his posture. "Thank you. It's important that you understand what you're defending. If this other company has a competitive system, so be it. But if this is just some bullshit to destroy my business, I want to gut them where they stand. This has been my life's work." He pointed to the monitor.

"Absolutely. If you don't mind, I'll go through the entire process to make sure I recognize what your people experience versus this other company. Oh and is there a computer here I can check out their website?"

"I have a clean laptop you can use. Give me a second." He returned to the keyboard and shut down access. "Come with me." They headed to the conference room. He unlocked a cabinet.

"Use this one," he said after turning it on and using the password.

"What's the name of the copycat company?"

He gave her the name and website address. For the next ten minutes, Melinda signed up for a job as an E&E, downloaded the contract, and downloaded the training instructions sending her to Leo's offices. She downloaded everything she could from the competing site and gathered their domain information as well.

An hour and a half later, armed with the light of battle in her eyes, Leo escorted Melinda to the car. The ride to her house was different than the one to the office. She asked questions and made notes, discussing the business the entire drive.

When Timms pulled into her driveway, Leo walked her to the door and stepped inside.

"Thanks this has been—"

He wrapped his arm around her and kissed her hard. Hesitating for a second, she wrapped her arms around his neck and pulled him close. They broke apart on a gasp. Leo ran his thumb across her lower lip.

"Tomorrow, I'll send that retainer. One day soon I want to have breakfast with you after dinner. Right now both our plates are full. I'm making room on mine. I hope you do the same." He placed a quick kiss on her lips and walked out the door.

Chapter 13

The next morning the parking lot had been full of job applicants. Security called police when people wouldn't leave and demanded payment. Some threw food at the building. Others left trash everywhere. Up until the time the police arrived, Leo had thought the mob outside would storm his building. He took extra precautions with his computer system, made sure everything was backed up into the cloud and another remote location.

Tenants on the first floor complained to the managing company about the disturbance in the parking area. Neighbors complained about the traffic. The news showed up, interviewed the applicants, and ran the story before he arrived to work.

Melinda, God bless her, fired back against the news station so fast they backtracked with an apology under threat of a lawsuit for not doing their due diligence. He and the staff had been instructed not to speak to the press, she'd handle everything, but her intervention may have come too late.

When he arrived this morning, a client had called to cancel a surveillance job. Somehow they were afraid their client would recognize one of the people from the parking lot. He'd written a withdrawal letter for the RFP with every intention of sending it, but couldn't. Submitting the damn thing had been his decision and he'd deal with the fall-out.

Leo's phone beeped, he read the caller ID, and headed to his office.

"Thompson?" Leo said.

"One second," Thompson said.

Leo nodded, realized he couldn't be seen, and paced his office floor for a few more minutes.

"Leo?"

He closed his office door and sat on the corner of his desk. "Thompson?" *Please say the bid's awarded to someone else and this is all over*, he prayed.

"Just called to check on you. How are things? I've got two jobs I'm sending you this week."

That helped some. "Other than a copycat company trying to drive me out of business, everything's good. Any way they can speed up that award, get these jokers off my back?"

"Copycat? Hmm, I'm not surprised. Although, haven't heard of that one being used in a while. I'm sorry you and your employees are going through this. Lately it seems to be a part of the process unfortunately. Everything you turned in looks good. If you can keep your nose clean for another week, I don't see why you won't receive the contract."

No, no, no. I don't want it. "I can't be the lowest bid."

"Just stay out of trouble. Your methods of securing information in real time are unsurpassed. You've spent thousands of hours developing your intelligence system. Don't forget that. It's an excellent program that several other agencies need to experience. Another week and this will be done."

"Thanks for the pep talk, I needed it, and thanks for the additional work," Leo said, rather than snorting his disbelief and offending a paying client.

"You're welcome. Like I said, I'm sorry that you're going through this, but it'll be over soon."

"Will it? If I win the contract these guys will play nice, leave me in peace to do the job? Or continue to undermine my company? Isn't their goal to get this contract? If that's the case, they can shoot for it if I fail to deliver, so I don't see them stopping if I win the contract."

"That's one way to look at it I suppose."

"Give it to them," Leo said, releasing a weight from his shoulders. "I'm not ready to expand, especially now that my company is under attack. I won't be able to fulfill the conditions of the contract."

Silence greeted his request. "I can't get involved and change my position at this point, but I won't push your company any more. That's the best I can do."

"Thank you, I really appreciate it. I will expand, but at a slower pace. Virginia is next, then South Carolina. You'll have first dibs, I promise," Leo said, uncertain if telling Thompson his plans was the best strategy, but he needed to give the man something.

"Great, that would be excellent. The agencies under my direction will continue to use you as an additional layer of intelligence. It's made a difference already," Thompson said in a lighter tone. After a few other things they disconnected.

Barb knocked on the door. "Everyone's here."

Leo stood and headed toward the conference room where his trained decoys and staff were seated for a meeting. He glanced at his watch. Melinda said she'd try to make the meeting to explain their strategy going forward. She arrived when he was halfway through his narrative explaining the bid contract and what happened afterward. When he finished, he introduced her to the group.

Denise and Stacy, pre-law students, asked a few questions regarding the legality of what the rogue company had done. Melinda answered every question thoroughly, leaving no question in his mind and perhaps those of the others that she was on top of the situation.

By the end of the meeting the heavy fog of uncertainty lifted from his shoulders. He'd agreed to meet Tag, Craig, and Derrick for drinks at a nearby bar that afternoon. Barb and a few others said they might join them. They were united in their disgust at the bidding process, the rogue company, and anyone who supported it. His team stood behind the company and agreed the setbacks were temporary. The announcement of the two new jobs was met with cheers and fist bumps.

He walked Melinda to her car and spoke to security on the way. "Any problems today?" Leo asked.

"No. A couple showed up this afternoon, but nothing after that. The news has been all over themselves getting the story straight. That helped," Timms said.

Leo smiled at Melinda. "I should've come to you the first day. You've handled this thing in less than twenty-four hours."

"You have a week to go. Consider this round one, but it's not over by a long shot, especially if you really have a shot at winning the contract." She looked at him as she pushed the button to unlock her car. "If what that guy told you is true, expect this week to be worse. I'm not saying this to discourage you, but I want you prepared for anything."

He stared down into concerned, dark blue eyes. "Thank you, I'll do my best."

A cheeky smile rose on her face. "I'm counting on that. Now use that brain of yours to track this bastard down. Follow the money."

"Yes, ma'am." He smiled and watched her drive off.

Chapter 14

Later that evening around six o'clock, Leo and Craig worked on beefing up security at the office by adding rooftop cams with views capable of expanding three blocks. They'd just finished testing the additional hardware and sat with a cold drink talking in the reception area. In fifteen minutes they'd meet Tag and Derrick at the bar for drinks.

A string of pooping sounds, and the window cracking sounded through the building.

"What the hell?" Leo hit the ground and looked to make sure Craig was okay. *Guns*?

When he didn't hear any more noise, he ran toward the back near his office. Of course something would happen the one time he convinced Jackson's security guy to go grab a bite to eat because he'd missed both meals earlier. Craig followed.

Five bullet holes dotted one of the back windows near the coffee and supply area. His cell phone vibrated, alerting him of the security breach and the security alarm rang in the building. Leo pulled out his phone and turned off the alarm.

He stared at the small holes. Blood rushed and pounded in his ears at the sight of the webbed glass surrounding each puncture. *What if someone had been in this area? Craig? Cherise?* His face heated as his hands clenched and unclenched. They'd lost their fucking minds. Turning, he ran to the console room and pulled up the remote camera and replayed the last few minutes. A silver SUV. He zoomed in on the license plate and verified it was the same five guys from a few days before.

"What the fuck just happened?" Craig yelled, running into the room.

Leo didn't answer.

Heart beat racing, he widened his search for the SUV using the remote cams on the roof until he caught sight of it heading toward the highway. The SUV stopped at the red light a couple blocks from the office.

Determined to make the motherfucker pay, he opened the network. "Eyes on, everybody. Here's the license plate of the silver SUV that just sprayed the office with bullets and ran like a fucking cockroach," Leo said in a blanket announcement, preparing to activate decoys nearby to find the bastards. He flipped on audio and the side monitors to display as many cameras at a time as possible.

"All ears and eyes on deck. Find the bitch, call it in so we can track his movement. Last seen turning at a stop light at the intersection of Greer and Independence. Anybody out there?" Tapping fingertips on the console, he waited to hear reports as green lights lit all over the area.

"Yeah, that's more like it." His gaze flitted all over the board. Some decoys were too far away so he restricted their access, returning their lights to blue. "Come on, come on, don't let that bastard get away ..." Leo murmured, staring at the screen.

"Give me that plate again?" somebody asked.

"NC tag number LWD998," Leo said and then repeated the make and model.

"Got a sighting on High Point Rd, just passed, heading east."

"Yes," Leo shouted. He accepted the transmission and a video of a similar SUV appeared on the screen.

"I need eyes and ears on High Point Rd. Verify sightings if possible follow." Leo's heart raced as he glanced at the green dots on another screen. "Call the police. Get me

Jackson's friend, Detective Bronson," Leo said over his shoulder to Craig.

"I see it and following," someone said. A few seconds later a video of the SUV turning into the large mall parking lot filled the screen.

"Denise and I are in the mall," Stacy said. "Which side is he on?"

"Looks like he's heading to the parking deck. I need more eyes at the mall. Anyone in that vicinity?" Leo zoomed into the mall location. There were so few dots he was tempted to drive over there himself. He released a breath as several green dots moved in that direction.

"That detective guy's not in," Craig said. "I left a message on his voice mail about the shooting and to call you—"

Leo's phone rang. He looked at the caller ID and answered. "Detective."

"Someone shot into your building?" Bronson asked.

"One second," Leo said to the detective and placed the phone on the console.

"I see the truck!" Stacy yelled. "He's going all the way to the top. Anybody up there?"

"Yeah. I'm here waiting for the bastard." Leo looked at the ID of the speaker and smiled. Tag and Derrick were supposed to meet them later, but obviously Tag got some shopping done first.

"Cameras and videos only, do not engage. I want someone on every level following this guy. If he gets into another car, I want eyes on the plate. Eyes on every exit and on the roads. Let's find this sucker and get him locked away." Leo leaned forward, his gaze flew from one screen to the other, looking for a glimpse of the guys who shot up his building.

Leo looked at the phone, remembered the detective, and answered, "Yes. No one was hurt. But I'm tracking the truck who did it."

"What? You got eyes on it?"

"Yes. The truck just turned into the mall and it looks like they're parking in the deck." He gave the detective the license tag information and description of the vehicle.

"Are these the same guys Jackson told me about, the ones who came to your office before?"

"The license plates match," Leo told Bronson while listening to the decoys report the status of the SUV.

"Son of a bitch parked and is walking toward the stairs. Looks about six feet, maybe a little less. Bastard's hiding his face," Tag said, the anger in his voice flowed through the speaker as an image followed by video footage flashed on screen.

The person leaving the SUV wore a heather gray hoodie and jeans. He walked with a masculine gait to the stairs with his head down. Leo couldn't tell if he wore sunglasses or not. Somebody took a picture of his face in the stairwell as they passed.

Leo frowned. This wasn't one of the guys who came to his office. White male with dark hair and deep set dark eyes, could be Latino or Middle Eastern. At least now they had a face.

"He didn't come to the next level. He may be on his way down to the first floor," someone said.

Leo updated the detective and everyone at the mall. The number of decoys had increased to eighteen.

"Tell your people to back off. We'll take it from here," Bronson said.

"He just walked out on the first floor and is in the crosswalk going into the mall." Another picture of the male flashed on the screen. The guy had removed his hoodie and looked like a college professor with a short sleeved shirt tucked in a pair of Dockers.

"He's coming toward you, Stacy," Leo said, ignoring Bronson.

"On it," she said. Her camera came online, and Leo watched as she and Denise looked at store items.

"He's coming up behind you," Leo told her. His gaze locked on the screen.

Stacy stepped back and bumped into him. Her long blond hair brushed against his chest as she looked up at him. He reached out to steady her, and she smiled up at him while Denise recorded at a distance.

"I'm so sorry." She held onto his arm.

"No problem." He released her and went to step aside.

Stacy stepped in the same direction. "Oops, sorry," she said, her cheeks reddening as she smiled.

He smiled and waved. "Ladies first."

Arrogant bastard. Leo couldn't believe how calm that son of a bitch acted after what he'd just done. The custom-made windows in his office were expensive and designed to prevent anyone from breaking into the building and tampering with his computer system. It could be days before the window could be replaced. Son-of-a-bitch would pay for it one way or the other.

Stacy nodded, turned, and walked in the opposite direction. Denise followed a few feet behind him, her phone to her ear while the video recorded his moves. When he headed for the exit, she remained in the store.

"I've got him outside," three different voices said as Leo received transmissions from various angles.

The guy stopped at navy blue mid-size car, and pressed his remote. Leo zeroed in on the license number and then pulled back just in time to see an unmarked police car pull up behind him. Bronson stepped out with his gun pointed at the guy.

"Can I get ears on this?" Leo asked through the microphone.

"They aren't talking loud enough and I can't get any closer," a decoy said.

Leo laughed when the target's mouth dropped open as he stared at Bronson and the other police as they pulled up and boxed him in. The man knelt on the ground with his hand on the back of his head while Bronson cuffed and escorted him to the back of the car.

Another monitor showed the cops surround the silver SUV in the parking lot. Leo leaned back in his seat, his eyes flitting from screen to screen. When Bronson drove off with the perp, the ton of pressure lodged between his eyebrows lifted.

Craig had been leaning against the desk in silence since the detective returned the call. "How long did all of that take?"

"Huh?" Leo looked over his shoulder.

"From the time we heard the shots to the time they arrested him? How long did all of that take?"

Leo leaned back and gave the matter thought. "I'm not sure. An hour?" He couldn't recall the exact time he heard the shots, but it wasn't seven yet, the sun hadn't fully set.

"Try a little over thirty minutes," Craig said, his grin widening. "That was fucking epic! Did you see how everybody stepped up and caught that bastard?"

Adrenaline rush over, Leo rubbed his forehead and nodded. "It worked. We got him."

"Leo?" Jackson called out from somewhere in the office.

"In here," Leo said, thinking about everything that just happened. In retrospect their response time had been awesome.

"Why did Bronson call me about the shots instead of you?" Jackson asked looking down at him. Timms followed and stood near the door, his arms across his chest.

Leo met Jackson's scowl with a frown of his own. "I don't know. Honestly, I just reacted. I didn't want the bastard to get away, and I didn't want my people to approach them."

"Them?" Jackson asked.

"At the time I thought it was the five guys from the other day. Turns out it's the same license plate but a different guy driving," Leo said. The whole security thing was too new to register as an immediate thing he should do in a crisis but looking at Jackson's scowling features, now wasn't the time to say that.

Jackson held his gaze for a few minutes and then nodded. "Fast thinking. This could be the break we need to put a stop to this. Whoever hired this guy crossed a line. I'll be honest, there are probably three people between this guy and the people paying for everything. But this is a good start."

Good start? Leo couldn't imagine anything good coming out of gunshots being fired at his building. Fortunately most of the tenants on the first floor had left for the day or he'd have additional vacancies to add to his growing list of problems.

"Bronson will try to get some information from the guy, but he'll probably lawyer up. The recording of the car and the license plate and photo of him leaving the car is golden. Bronson will stop by later for a statement and to see what you have."

"Thanks," Leo looked at Timms. "I convinced Brown to go grab a bite to eat. We had a flare up earlier and he missed eating all day. I didn't want him to pass out. That's why he's not here."

"I know, he got my permission before he left," Timms said.

"Oh. Great."

"How long do you think it took to catch that guy?" Craig asked, his voice brimming with excitement as if he'd drank a dozen of those little bottles of energy.

Jackson's gaze slid from Craig to Leo and then back to Craig. "How long?"

"Little over thirty minutes from the time we heard the shots." Craig said it so fast the words bunched together.

"Slow down. Thirty minutes?"

Grinning, Craig nodded several times. His eyes sparkled as if he'd just revealed the world's closest held secret.

Jackson whistled and looked at Leo. "Impressive. You got him leaving the parking lot?"

Leo nodded and then placed two fingertips to his forehead to calm the bass drum beating inside his skull. A blanket of tiredness rested on his shoulders, inhibiting his movements, slowing down his thoughts. Moments before, his fingers raced across the keyboard. Now, he could barely lift his hand. He didn't want to talk, not to Jackson anyway.

"Mind if I get a look at that window?" Jackson asked.

Eyes closed, Leo waved him and Timms to the back.

"Tag and Derrick are on their way here instead of the bar. If you feel up to it we'll go later," Craig said.

Leo waved his fingers and allowed his thoughts to drift for a few moments while he rested.

"We totally kicked ass today," Craig said.

"It was epic. I hope we do more work like that, seems we're built to deal with that kind of shit," Tag said.

"Can't believe that son of a bitch shot up the office. What if someone had gotten hurt?" Derrick said.

Leo groaned, identifying everyone's voice.

"You okay?" Derrick asked, placing a hand on Leo's shoulder.

"Yeah, yeah, just grabbed a quick nap. Tired for some reason." He wiped his mouth with the back of his hand, sat up, and looked at the monitor. Blue dots were everywhere. He frowned. They'd been a sea of green before.

"I closed out that last call," Craig said.

Grateful he wouldn't need to pay decoys when he didn't need them, Leo nodded. "Thanks, I appreciate it."

Craig grinned and rocked on his heels. "Jackson left. Timms is downstairs. The detective wants you to call him when you can."

"Thanks." Leo pushed up on the console, typed in a few keys to run a scan, and headed to his office. "You guys go ahead. I need to fill out a police report for the insurance to fix the window. Might take me some time."

"We'll wait," Derrick said, following him down the hall.

Leo looked at him over his shoulder, noticed the dogged glint in his eye, and shook his head slightly. When they entered his office, Leo looked at Derrick. "I don't feel like going. Tonight, I'd like to eat and rest, not hang out at a bar."

Derrick's hand flew to his chest. His eyes widened. "I'm shocked. Truly shocked that you're bailing at the last minute since you've always gone to hang out with us before," he finished with a cynical twist to his lips.

Leo chuckled at Derrick's sarcasm. "No doubt I earned that, but can I get a rain check? I promise we'll get together soon."

"No problem, whatever you need." Derrick extended his balled fist.

Leo bumped it and watched Derrick leave. He moved to stand in front of the closed circuit cameras and watched the three leave the parking lot.

Chapter 15

A few minutes afterward Leo and Timms were the only ones in the building. Leo started a fresh pot of coffee and drank a bottle of water. When the coffee finished brewing, he poured a large mug and headed into his office to run checks on the license plates of the SUV and the blue car in the parking lot.

Ramon Delgado used his ex-wife's credit card for the rented vehicles last week. Leo's security clearance and information from the FBI database allowed him to delve deeper into Delgado's life. Within two hours he amassed a wealth of knowledge about the former Cub Scout leader who fired shots into his building. Delgado drove from South Carolina to Greensboro because someone told him to, a job, nothing more.

Within the past week Delgado, his ex-wife, his sister, and his parents each deposited twenty-five hundred cash into their bank accounts on two separate days. That made a hefty amount just under twenty-five thousand for the entire family. *Interesting.* As he went through the family's financial accounts for the past twelve months, he saw three separate instances where all five made high-dollar cash deposits around the same time. Is this how Delgado cleaned his payments? Or was he just generous? Maybe the entire family had something to do with these jobs.

"According to Jackson, you'd be the bottom layer and someone the IRS would love to chat with," Leo murmured, looking at several pictures of Delgado and his family.

Leo wanted a name and the reason why he'd been attacked. He cracked his knuckles and prepared a spoof email from the bank to send each of Delgado's family members, informing them of a problem. He attached a pesky virus he'd created in college that would replicate and at various times hide critical information for several seconds. In twelve hours it would begin deleting files.

In a couple days he'd send a note to the local IRS field agent, accusing the Delgado family of money laundering. Nothing rattled the government's cage like folks hiding taxable income.

Leo took a bite from his apple and pressed enter. The damage inflicted on the Delgado clan would have them in tears by the end of the week. Less than Ramon deserved for shooting at the building and orchestrating the visit by the five thugs. Unfortunately, Leo couldn't find anything to tie Delgado to the copycat company but suspected the man was involved.

Someone tapped on his door. He wasn't in the mood to talk or make excuses for not wanting to talk, so he didn't answer.

The door opened.

Jackson and another man stepped inside.

His gaze flicked over the slender stranger and then at Jackson. Leo hit a few keystrokes to save his information and shut it down before anyone recognized the logo of the restricted website. Thompson had cleared Leo's access to several federal databases to work the jobs assigned, not to make the Delgados cry. Jackson introduced Detective Bronson before sitting in one of the chairs in front of the desk. Jackson and Bronson were similar in height, but that's the only thing they had in common. Bronson's jet black hair and tawny-colored eyes seemed to sweep up everything in a single glance, contrasted with Jackson's blue eyes and blonde hair.

"Got a minute?" Jackson asked.

Since they'd barged in, Leo nodded and leaned back in his chair. "What can I do for you?"

Bronson leaned forward. "I'm not quite sure what type business you're running. Students apply for jobs and you what? Train them to be detectives? To go out on jobs against criminals?"

Leo didn't bother looking at Jackson who sat in the other chair. "No, not as detectives. Anyone can apply for a job here. Students aren't the only staff we hire. Housewives, people looking for part-time work, anybody with the right aptitude for a particular job can be trained as you're aware."

Bronson nodded. "True, but seems like mostly college students on your payroll."

Leo shrugged. "Flexible training, irregular work, higher than average and weekly pay isn't for everyone."

"Sounds like a commercial," Bronson said as he sat back in the chair.

"That's an idea," Jackson said, joining the conversation.

"We arrested the bastard who fired a weapon into your building. He won't talk, even with his attorney present. Not that it matters. We got his prints in the SUV and pictures of him driving and exiting the vehicle." He nodded to Leo. "Thanks for your cooperation in sharing the information. I'll need copies of the tape from the cameras and any other information you have."

"No problem," Leo said, hoping Bronson would get to the purpose of his visit.

"Noticed a lot of students at the mall taping everything, even when we asked them to step away, they backed up but didn't leave. They did that because this guy shot your place?" Bronson asked.

"Or to get paid for submitting information," Leo said.

Bronson chuckled. "How do you know who's gets paid and who doesn't? That seems like a lot of work that could turn ugly if you make a mistake."

"Been at it for a while, haven't shorted anyone yet."

"That network you have, it came in handy, wouldn't have caught Delgado without it. Good deal."

"Delgado?" Leo asked Bronson, proud his voice held the right mixture of ignorant curiosity.

"That's the guy we arrested. Do you mind if I record your statement?"

"No, that'd be faster." He repeated the entire ordeal in a detached voice, removing his emotions from the horror of the day. When he finished, Bronson asked a few questions and then looked at the video of the shooting.

Leo gave the detective a copy of the tape and a few still photos. He waited for them both to leave so he could go home and rest.

"Remember you said I could use your resources to assist me in my cases?" Jackson said.

Leo wanted to scream at the delays. Instead, he smiled at Jackson and nodded. "Sure you need something?"

"I just got this case from an insurance company to tail this guy for possible theft."

Leo held up his hand. "If that's the Graham case there could be a conflict. I received an email this evening that they canceled the contract with our firm. I haven't even pulled Griff off it yet." He held up a finger and placed the call.

When he hung up, Griff was on his way home. "Okay, that's done. We had a tracker on Graham's car. I'll disable it."

Jackson's gaze bore into him. "Listen, I didn't know you had that case."

Frowning, Leo looked at him. "Why would you know that?"

"I just didn't want you to think I went behind your back and took something from you," Jackson said, his tone low, his gaze serious.

"No problem. It's not the first case I've lost since this started." *Just the last civilian paying one.* He exhaled and looked at Jackson. "What do you need?"

He pulled a picture from his pocket and handed it to Leo. "Graham met with this man tonight in the bathroom at the strip club. They've met two nights this week. I'd like to get eyes and ears on him."

Leo looked at the photo, his brow rose. "I know this guy. He's a former client."

Jackson leaned forward. "Stephen Carter?"

"Yeah. That's him. He was with Graham?" No wonder the insurance company cancelled their contract. Griff had been trailing Graham for two weeks and never reported any bathroom meetings.

"The past two nights."

Leo returned the photo and pushed away the voice inside his head, mocking his company for terrible surveillance work. He'd deal with Griff tomorrow when he gave the man his final check. "What do you need?" He straightened in his chair.

Jackson's gaze flitted between Bronson and Leo before he answered. "There's a discrepancy in Carter's records. I can't determine what's going on between him and Graham until I get answers."

"Okay," Leo said after a few minutes of silence.

"Stephen Carter … doesn't exist. Not anywhere. Except at special moments like meeting Graham, a suspected jewel thief, in a strip club."

"Or walking into my office to order services," Leo added. His brow rose meaningfully.

"I found no record of Stephen Carter. No marriage or driver's license. No military ID or credit cards or social security. In the system he does *not* exist."

Leo leaned back. His thoughts flipped two weeks back when Carter came to the office. At the time Leo thought the man had a weird fashion sense because he wore a long sleeved jacket when outside temperatures were in the high 80s. But once they discussed the job and signed the contract he hadn't given it much thought.

"Again, what do you need?" Leo asked.

"To verify who he is," Jackson said.

"How can decoys do that?" Leo was curious just how far Jackson thought he'd go to repay a debt. Not far enough to have decoys verify the sexuality of a former client that's for sure.

No one said anything.

"Sorry, nothing I can do on that score. It's not against the law to cross-dress," Bronson said, standing.

Jackson's phone beeped. He held up his hand, stopping Bronson while watching Leo and listening to whoever was on the phone. "When did Carter hire you?" he asked Leo after disconnecting.

"One sec." Leo turned on the computer and looked through his records. "The nineteenth of this month."

Bronson's eyes widened as he sat down. "When did you do the job for him?"

Leo's gaze flicked between the two men before looking at his record. "One night surveillance and decoy work with his wife at a club on the twenty-first."

Bronson cleared his throat and pinched the bridge of his nose. "On the night of the twenty-first, the victim, a call girl, went missing. Her body was found the next day in an alley on Main in Winston-Salem. Witness' description placed the victim with Graham around midnight. Several people verified

Graham had been in the club at that time." He paused, looked at Jackson and then Leo.

"This girl had been seen with Carter's wife on numerous occasions. According to Mrs. Carter, she severed the relationship on the twenty-first when she met someone else she preferred earlier that night." Bronson's eyes lit. "When I questioned them, Carter and Graham claimed not to know each other."

"Yet, they've been meeting each other at the club the past few nights," Jackson said.

"Point made, Jacks. I'll bring them both in," Bronson said.

Jackson stood, holding up his phone. "Better call it in. Carter and Graham just headed to the airport."

Bronson and Jackson stood and left.

Leo stared at the empty door way a few seconds, praying the Carter case wouldn't bite him in the ass. His phone beeped and a yellow light flashed on a panel embedded on his desk.

"Fuck, why can't this day just die?" He pulled out his keyboard and entered the necessary codes. Someone had tried to access his program and fell into one of his traps

Chapter 16

Not only did the Carter case kick the company in the ass, it exploded like at two ton bomb because of Griff's shoddy work. The insurance company wrote a heated letter demanding a refund for the past week, which Leo agreed to do.

Carter lawyered up and threatened to sue Leo for divulging confidential information, even though he hadn't. Other than admit the man had been a client and the date they worked for Carter, Leo hadn't revealed anything. He hoped Bronson hadn't thrown him beneath the bus with lies to get Carter to talk.

Worse, Miller, Brown, and Graves—Melinda's firm— returned his retainer and cancelled their services, claiming Graham had been a previous client and there'd be conflict of interest now that they handled both Graham and Carter cases.

Melinda hadn't known until afterward and threatened to quit because of their greed and unprofessionalism. She swore dollar signs moved the partners, not protocol. Leo thought she should remain at the law firm since she had spent months searching for a job in her field. An hour of going back and forth she agreed to remain, but promised she'd either represent him if it came to that or he'd get her approval on a replacement first.

He accepted the compromise.

Griff arrived shortly after they opened and offered no real excuse other than he never thought to follow Graham into the john. He refused to believe Graham had done anything beneath his nose until Bronson showed up an hour later to question him.

That's when things got real.

Bronson questioned Stacy, Barb, and Denise about that night in the club with the victim, Lillian Drake. His search warrant granted him the right of the videos from that night at Lingerie and all surveillance on Graham.

Leo's face burned with shame as he listened to Griff, a former police detective, make excuses for doing such poor work. Bronson tore into him, reminding him of basic procedures. When Bronson finished with Griff, the guy sat in the chair with his head hanging low. Leo tried to summon sympathy for the older man and couldn't. The dark stain of incompetence placed on the company would take years to recover.

"You don't have to pay me for that job. The others, Derrick and Tag, they shadowed him at the hotel, went inside, watched his room, they earned their pay. Keep mine, I didn't earn it," Griff said.

Silently Leo agreed and retrieved the company equipment from Griff before releasing him from employment. Griff waved to Cherise and Barb as he left the office. Timms escorted Griff to his car.

Chest heavy, Leo strode to his office and slammed the door. How'd his company get mixed up in a murder investigation? Jackson claimed Carter may have used the company to cover their tracks, but that didn't explain the murder or how any of the pieces of the puzzle worked or if he verified the information on Carter that he needed.

Leo looked over his accounts and readjusted his thinking on their financial outlook. Three potential clients sent emails this morning changing their minds. One requested the return of his deposit. Things weren't dire but with the loss of those upcoming jobs, and refunding the insurance company their fees, it would be tight for a while.

For the first time since he submitted, he hoped they won the bid. The extra padding would ease the financial burdens and keep them in the black. Otherwise he'd dip into his personal savings.

Bronson hadn't said anything else about Delgado. Leo placed a call to Jackson. "What's the deal with the guy who shot up my building?"

"Ask Bronson. I don't have anything to do with that," Jackson said.

Leo chuckled.

"What?"

"Last night, the stuff you knew about Carter, Graham … you've been digging deep in a database that holds a lot of secrets. I ran Carter this morning, his fake shit held. To get what you had requires a different level of security."

"And you discuss this with me on the phone?" Jackson said, his tone dry.

"Good point. I'll make an appointment. When's a good time?"

"Give me a couple hours. We can talk then," Jackson said.

Leo clicked off and checked his emails. Two jobs from Thompson sat in the queue. *Thank God.* He reviewed each one and set them up in the system. The pay for both of these would keep them in the black a couple months at least. By then the whole bid thing would be over and they could put all of this behind them.

One order dealt with a similar job before, to keep a female target occupied for a certain length of time. Thompson sent a detailed bio on the female, her like of younger, athletic men, preferably exotic. She wasn't above paying for a good time either. This job went live in less than forty-eight hours. He'd go over it with Barb and then see who was available.

The next job was surveillance for a target arriving in two days. Leo searched for information on the woman first. Thompson called before he finished.

"What happened?" Thompson demanded.

"What do you mean?" Dread rolled down his back and merged with shame, an alien feeling regarding his business until today.

"Did Hotsel Insurance hire your company to run a surveillance job on a mark?"

How had he found out about that? "Yes."

"Yes? Is it true another investigation company cracked the case while your operative sat in the same club with the target, oblivious to what was going on in the place?"

Leo leaned forward, his forehead resting in the palm of his hand.

"And the investigation company is the same company you included in your proposal?" Thompson asked, the tone of his voice whiplash thin.

"Yes and yes," Leo said, turning from the two orders they'd now lose. *Shit.*

"You wanted out of the contract? Consider it done. You lost the award with that stunt. But, that wasn't the way to go about it. You made me appear foolish for recommending you."

"Seriously? I'd never make myself look this bad to get out of a contract. The op on that job, former detective, solid twenty years' experience. He missed it this time, his credentials are top notch."

A breath of silence followed his comments.

"Hmm, in that case, somebody got to him. Paid him off to mess up your name, your business. That whole deal went down late last night, yet when I arrived this morning a brief with details was on my desk and the entire committee received the same report. Sure we vet and scrutinize contractors, but someone wanted to make sure the committee knew about this before they make their decision tomorrow."

"Tomorrow? I thought it was next week?"

"I didn't want you to worry so I stretched it out." Thompson paused. "You got the jobs I sent?"

"Yes." Was Thompson going to cancel those too?

"Good, get on it. Any questions?"

Surprise over Thompson's continued faith stole his vocabulary. Leo cleared his throat. "No, not at this point. I'll sit down with my team and develop a plan."

"Watch who you talk to. Not everyone's on your team."

"I see." His thoughts short-circuited over Thompson's declaration. Who? Three other people worked full time: Cherise, Barb, and Craig. It was inconceivable that any of them betrayed him.

"Keep the woman busy for a short while until you get clearance to back off."

"No problem."

"The second one, Oscar Blevins, is the one I need eyes and ears on. For him to be so close, we need to find out what he's up to. It's rare for him to visit the states and even though there's no proof of his crimes, he's rumored to have sold classified documents on the black market and financed terrorist activities in the Middle East."

"Okay." This was the first time Thompson explained an assignment which surprised Leo. He pulled up the Blevins job and looked at a picture of the target.

"Activate as many decoys as you need," Thompson continued. "I want pictures of him in restaurants, the hotel, and anyone he comes in contact with. You have a larger budget with this, same terms with half deposited when you accept the job. Oh and keep that detective, the one who visited your office today, out of the loop. No need to involve the locals."

Leo's head snapped up. He looked at the phone. "How'd you know that?"

Thompson didn't answer. "Get me verifiable information on what Blevins is up to within a twenty-four hour window after he arrives."

"Verifiable information? You want sources? How detailed? Turnaround?" They'd need to work fast to get this one done.

"Yes, yes, a very detailed report, highlights of his visit while he's there, and a full report within five hours after he leaves. This is a quick assignment. We believe he'll be in and out, activate your team now to go on this."

"The clock starts now even though he won't be here for forty-eight hours?"

"No, he'll be in Greensboro *within* forty-eight hours. He could arrive any time now. I'll send you a text when he's en route."

"Got it." Leo disconnected. He called Barb and gave her the information on the case but didn't tell her they'd lost the bid. He planned to hold that close for a while. Losing the bid didn't bother him as much as having a snake in his house.

Chapter 17

Determined to get answers, Leo arrived at Jackson's office and introduced himself to the receptionist who ushered him down a short, unadorned hallway to a half-opened door. Jackson sat at a large wood desk, talking on the phone, and looked up at Leo's approach.

"A client just walked in. I need to speak with him. We'll talk later when I get home." Jackson disconnected and motioned for him to close the door.

Leo shut it and sat in the leather bucket chair in front of the desk. Neither of them spoke for a few seconds.

"Who's trying to destroy my business? Is this more than the bid?" Leo asked, the need to know made his tone curt. At first he thought Delgado, but the man was still in custody. Fuller hadn't been seen in the area, but that didn't mean he wasn't somewhere pulling strings. There had to be someone else.

"It could be. I'm not sure if somebody else hopped on board the screw Grit, Inc. train, or the other bidders want to make sure you never compete again, or how deep the shit goes. But this Carter thing is over the top."

"Did you find out what you needed about Carter?"

Jackson waved down the question. "Yeah, that's settled, the Mister is female."

Leo blinked a couple times. "Mr. & Mrs. Carter are both women?"

"Surgery. That's all I can say."

"Who sent Delgado?" Leo asked, leaning forward.

"I'm not sure. He's not talking."

Leo tilted his head and continued staring at Jackson. "Last week someone gave Delgado $25K … cash. This week thugs use his SUV to check out my company. Then he uses an automatic to redecorate my building. I'd say he's talking."

Jackson eyes bored into his for a few seconds. "I told you these players play for keeps. It's a different arena."

Leo nodded, remembering their last conversation. "True, but there's a snake in my house. I can't operate like that. I have to flush it out, exterminate it," Leo said in a measured tone. Speaking the words released wisps of toxic anger that simmered since Thompson's call. Leo hadn't felt anger this intense, this gut-burning since his program, Venom, had been stolen. He was fully prepared to step into the dark arena of hacking he'd sworn off in college to learn the truth.

"I see." Jackson leaned forward. "I handle a little cyber-security as you know, in addition to armed services. Nowadays one dictates the use of the other. Intelligence, information is big business and whether you admit it or not, you're in a different league now. Thirty minutes from crime to capture? Clean, no casualties, an arrest that'll hold up in court? Man, you have no idea what you've done." He shook his head slightly and pointed at Leo.

"Why'd you get in this business?" Jackson asked.

"What?" The question threw him.

"Answer that question before we go any further."

"The challenge of creating a program that used common elements. Each day it's something new, the things I see through the eyes of the decoys. The places they go and share. It's amazing, liberating in a way." His face warmed from revealing such personal thoughts. He continued staring at Jackson. "What does that have to do with anything?"

"Everything. You lost a multimillion dollar contract that you were on track to win, at least that's what my sources say, and you're not upset about that. Your anger, which I'm happy to see by the way, is over someone attempting to steal your program and damaging your company name. Am I right?"

Leo waved his hand. "I'll expand, just not as fast. I always planned to do that."

"Why not let it go? Chances are the outside threats will stop and in time you'll repair your reputation," Jackson asked.

"No."

"No?" Jackson said when Leo didn't elaborate.

"No, I can't let this go. The insurance company will replace the window, but Delgado will remember this job for the rest of his life. A former employee left town. I'm tracking him now and when I find him, I'll deal with him as well."

Last night someone used the app he created for his decoys and attempted to attach a virus to an image during the time they tracked Delgado. He'd traced the app, terminated the connection and sent breach of contract notice to the former decoy. He sent Melinda the information to ask her opinion on his next move. The next time it happened he'd send a "fuck you" virus that would disable their phone as a parting gift.

"*Not everyone's on your team,*" Thompson had said. That comment spiraled deep. Griff left town two hours after Leo terminated him, prompting Leo to start extensive background checks on those closest to him. It broke his heart, but he needed to know.

"Whoa." Jackson held up his hands. "Do you know what you're doing? Going down certain paths stains you forever in ways you can never imagine." His voice deepened and Leo wondered if Jackson spoke from experience.

Leo looked at his fingers for a few seconds and then peered at Jackson. "For the most part I'm non-violent, at least physically. I don't do guns or anything, but I can ruin a person's life, make them wish they'd never seen my face or crossed me. I'll walk whatever path I need to discover if someone close betrayed me. They'll pay for that."

"Threat?"

"I figured you for a straight shooter."

Jackson's gaze narrowed. He stood, pulled a wand from his desk, stared at it, and tossed it back in. "If you're wired, this probably won't find the damn thing." He returned to his chair.

"I'm not wired." Leo leaned forward, elbows on his knees and fingertips pressed together. "So the thirty minute crime to capture episode … you say I have no idea what I've done. What about this? They're gunning for my ass to steal what I have and shut me down. Each time I complete a job for Thompson its money someone else isn't receiving. I get that."

Jackson pinned him with his steely gaze. "Do you? They will hire the best hackers money can buy to tear your program apart and rebuild it beneath their brand. If you'd won the contract … you'd get national recognition, it'd be harder to brush you aside. Now, they'll study what you've done, copy it, and incorporate it into their proposal. I guarantee you that a team has already been assigned to study and recreate your success."

Leo already figured that. If they could recreate Ghost or Venom, healthy competition moved the bar forward. But these guys didn't want competition at all, and that created a problem.

"Who's trying to destroy my business?" he asked again, meeting Jackson's gaze without flinching.

Jackson pursed his lips for a few seconds and then shrugged. "The consortium. A group of men who work together on government contracts. Started with five, down to three. Right now they manage over one hundred million dollars in government contracts."

Of course they do. It couldn't be one company with an egocentric CEO, Leo thought. "Is that a public corporation?"

Jackson's brow rose, and then he burst out laughing. When he could speak, he pointed at Leo again. "I like you. That was good." Moments later he sobered and leaned to the side of his chair. "Think legalized mafia and you'll get a picture of the consortium. They have lower level worker bees, like Delgado who know nothing about the guys at the top. Those bastards wear "pillars of the community" labels, head large million dollar corporations, make huge charitable donations and shit." He used his fingers for quotation marks. "The masks they wear are solid. Deposits are made into the pockets of politicians at the highest levels. For you … an unknown to enter the arena and take what they consider to be theirs was a bold step."

"Born of ignorance, I assure you," Leo muttered.

Jackson's lip curled into a semblance of a smile. "Gutsy. I'm not sure why Thompson put you up to it or what was his end game. He knew they'd never allow it. And when you asked for me to subcontract, it confused everyone no doubt. They probably thought we planned to take over the world." He laughed.

Leo frowned. "What did you have to do with this?"

Jackson's smile dimmed. "Mark works for me. I sent him to check you out."

Mark? Mark? The skateboarder? Leo recalled the former college student who'd done surveillance work for him in the past. He didn't use Mark as often since he graduated, but knew Mark kept in contact with Barb. "I knew he worked another job. He suggested your company to Barb as a good security company for part of the contract. You put him up to that?"

"No. But I wasn't surprised when he did." Jackson paused. "I gave your name to Thompson months ago. The first job you did for him had been assigned to my company. Based on what I'd learned about you, I realized you'd do a better job."

Leo stiffened as he processed Jackson's words. *Son of a bitch.* Jackson knew Thompson. His stomach clenched as pieces fell into place. They'd been watching him all along and he never had a clue.

"I asked Thompson a few times how he found my company. He never answered and I stopped asking. Should I say thank you?"

Jackson shrugged.

"You work for Thompson?" Leo asked, needing to know where everyone fit in on this crazy ride.

"Sometimes he uses my services, but I own my company."

Jackson wrote on a piece of paper and slid it to Leo. "The names on the top are the men in charge. The names on the second row are their attorneys and the ones who sign the contracts. The names on the last line are people they've used in the past to do dirty shit."

Leo read the list, none of the names meant anything to him. If company names were listed, he might get a better idea of who they were. But he'd find out everything about them soon.

Leo's phone beeped. He looked at the caller ID. *Melinda.* "Excuse me a second."

Jackson nodded.

"Hey, I'm in a meeting right now can I call you when I'm done?"

"Sure. That's fine. We need to talk," she said.

"Okay, I'll call you when I'm leaving." He disconnected and stared at the paper again. "I don't see Sam Fuller's name on this list." He looked at Jackson.

"Sam Fuller?" Jackson's voice deepened. "How do you know him?"

Leo told him what happened at the hotel after the bidding conference.

"First off, he didn't tell you his name. He would never do that, so you've been digging in dark places. Second, that's not like him to be so open. He's a behind the scenes guy, nasty." Jackson placed his fingertip against his lip and stared over Leo's head. "Okay. If Fuller is in this, that changes the game. It's more than cyber. There'll be some firepower as well. Looks like we'll be partners after all."

The calmly stated announcement drew Leo from staring at the list. "You know him?"

"Oh yeah, Sam and I have history and a promise. I owe him."

Chapter 18

Leo hung up from Melinda with a promise to meet her later tonight for dinner. As he pulled out of Jackson's parking lot, his mind hummed with plots and subplots swirling and tumbling over each other.

Jackson and Thompson. Carter and Graham. Bronson and the murder. He placed another call and after a brief conversation hung up, made a U-turn and pressed the gas pedal.

Ten minutes later he pulled into the parking lot of an industrial complex. Zeke worked in one of these buildings and they needed to talk.

His friend met him at the door with a one-armed hug and walked him past security into a lab. He waved his hand, pivoted, and smiled. "This is it. The place I work my magic. Behold and be amazed." He pulled out a long metallic paddle.

"What do you think this is?" He side-eyed Leo while twisting the paddle back and forth.

Leo stared at the device for a few moments. "A high-powered scanner?"

Zeke frowned. "No. Well, yes … but it does more than just scan. It also creates a barrier to stop future transmissions." He returned it to the shelf, picked up a bracelet, and held it up to the light. "Remember Xena? We used to watch her all the time at your place. This cuff is what I'm working on now. Once perfected, it will magnetize any metal projectiles directed at the wearer."

Leo took a step closer and stared. "This will stop bullets?"

"Eventually, I'm still working on it." He replaced it and looked at Leo over his shoulder. "How's your parents? Still in Tampa lying on the beach?"

"Yeah, Dad's living his dream retirement and Mom's riding shotgun," Leo said, looking around the lab. "What about your parents? Your brother?" he asked out of courtesy, unsure how to discuss his most recent problems with Zeke. It had been a few years since they'd spent time together.

"The parents are on one of those transatlantic cruises, and Bobby's in California with his girlfriend doing their thing." He shrugged. "You dating the woman you were with the other night?"

"Working on it," Leo said to make sure Zeke didn't get any ideas of talking to Melinda. No matter what happened between him and the attorney, she was off limits to Zeke. Leo took a moment to gather his words.

"Talked to a guy last week in the cave. He said no one's cracked Venom, claims he's been trying to modify it but couldn't. He asked if I knew who wrote it." Zeke's voice lowered at the end.

Hearing the name of his pet program jolted Leo out of his clouded thinking. Zeke and Nathan were the only two people who knew he'd created the virus that had been used against a major trading company. Some asshole from the cave used Venom against the company and wiped out millions of dollars in a day. Retirement funds, investments, everything. Stocks were bought and sold and then resold. It had been a vicious attack. Venom repopulated and contaminated every computer that logged on within the previous 30 days, deleting the data before cleaning up behind itself, leaving tracks that went nowhere.

In the hacker's underground a kiddie did a victory dance claiming he'd created Venom and shut down the trading company. Everyone knew the feds monitored those sites.

People committed suicide, lost their homes and even their businesses months after that meltdown. The punk was arrested and tried to change his story, but it was too late. The cops needed a fall guy and his boasts had been recorded.

Leo had spent hundreds of hours trying to perfect a way to control the virus with limited success and finally locked it away praying the cops wouldn't come after him.

"What'd you tell him?" Leo crossed his arms and met Zeke's gaze. The way the laws were written, it didn't matter that he hadn't been the one to use Venom. As the creator of the malicious virus designed to steal and destroy he was just as guilty.

"Same thing I said when we were in college. I don't know."

"You never should've taken it to the cave. It wasn't ready," Leo said, rehashing the argument that damaged their friendship several years ago.

During that time the Computer Crime and Intellectual Property Section (CCIPS) was on a witch hunt for the Coreflood botnet, which infected more than two million computers worldwide during the decade of its existence. The government left few stones unturned as they searched hacking forums for information on Coreflood and the Gameover Zeus Botnet. Both of these viruses spanned the globe, infecting computers, stealing millions of dollars from businesses and consumers. It was the worse time ever for Zeke to pull that stunt.

"I've apologized a million times," Zeke said, pulling out a stool and sitting with his shoulders hunched. "You'd won the bet, created a bug, I'd lost. Guess I wanted to see if anybody else could crack it, that's why I took it online to the cave." Zeke held up his hands, stopping Leo's scathing comeback. "I fucked up, caused a lot of problems, put us on the radar. I know. Water beneath the bridge so to speak. You need something now? Or just dropped by to catch up?"

Leo inhaled and then released a long breath. "Yeah. I do. But do me a favor and don't bring that shit up if you don't want me to go off. Still rips my gut when I think about the school's response to Venom and how fast I had to cover my tracks. If I'd been caught, they'd have sent me to priosn. If it's water under the bridge, leave it there. Deal?"

"Yeah, yeah, I hear you. No problem. It's all good. We cool," Zeke muttered as his gaze swept over the walls behind Leo.

"I need my office scanned," Leo said slowly, thinking through everything. Thompson and Jackson knew way too much about things going on in his office.

"Scanned?" Excitement rang in Zeke's voice.

"Yes," Leo drew out the one syllable, wondering who the snake in his office was.

Considering Griff's latest action, he topped the list except he rarely came into the office. Cherise had access to all administrative files, but couldn't access Ghost. Craig and Barb could monitor jobs on Ghost if he keyed them in, otherwise they were locked out. No one other than him had access to all the systems. Maybe Zeke might have some insight. They'd been thick in high school and college until he'd done that dumbass thing with Venom.

"I've got just what you need." Zeke moved about the lab, opening and closing drawers. "When do you want it done?"

"Tonight, after everyone's gone. Someone's talking, telling secrets in the office. I need to find out who." Tomorrow they'd start two new jobs, best to have this taken care of before then. Once the place was cleaned, he would go underground and do some serious tracking.

Zeke nodded. "No shit. That's fucked. Whatever you need, I've got your back."

Leo nodded. "You always did. I need a complete scan to clean my place." He wanted to make sure Zeke understood how serious he was.

"I can do that. Yeah, got just the thing." He pulled out a palm-sized device and held it up. "I didn't make this one, but it's powerful. If there's a bug in your building, this will find it. I can remove anything we find or short-circuit it, your choice." He placed the device in a leather case and looked at Leo.

"I hope there's nothing in the office, but whatever you find, you can keep, add to your research."

Zeke's smile brightened. "Sounds fair. What time should I get there?"

Leo had dinner with Melinda and would return to the office to make sure everything was ready for tomorrow. "Midnight should work. Come alone. I'll tell security to let you inside."

"That works. I planned to work late tonight anyway." Zeke paused, a concerned looked crossed his face. "You in some kind of trouble?"

Leo straightened, cleared his face, and forced a half smile. "No, new clients with higher security levels. I just need to stay on top of things."

The relief on Zeke's face touched Leo. "Makes sense. I've got some things you can use on your phone to make sure no one listens in. If they try, the only thing they hear is static."

"Thanks, man. I appreciate that." They bumped fists. Leo turned to leave. "See you tonight. Call me if something happens and you can't make it."

"Will do," Zeke said, walking him through security.

Chapter 19

Operation Find the Snake moved at a slow, steady pace. After spending hours researching each of his staff, not only did he know things about his employees that might haunt him forever, he was no closer to discovering who betrayed him.

Griff remained high on his list and when Leo returned to the office later, he hoped to find more information. He caught sight of Melinda sitting in the middle of the room. She raised her fingers and waved him over.

Inhaling, he strode to their table and smiled down into her eyes. "You are so beautiful." Over the past few days he'd come to believe she enjoyed his company and they were closer to spending intimate time together. Her reddening cheeks and bright smile confirmed he was right.

"I ordered you a sweet tea," she said, digging into her briefcase and pulling out a sheet of paper. "Delgado was charged, no surprise there. The DA is a friend of mine. She's trying to find out who hired him and may offer a plea bargain. He'll still serve time, but not as much. If that happens, I'll let you know."

"I thought your firm released me." He turned to the waiter and placed his order.

Melinda's smile reached her eyes. "They returned your retainer, but the copycat and Delgado case aren't closed and I'm still on them. Did you learn anything about Delgado?" She took a sip of her drink.

"Watch who you talk to, not everyone's on your team." Damn Thompson. "Yes, he was married, no kids, ex-wife lives in Charlotte. He's single right now, mostly basic stuff.

Works for a company that's not recorded anywhere." Leo shook his head, hoping she wouldn't push.

"He rented both vehicles using his ex-wife's credit card. Wonder if she knew he'd planned to stick her with a large bill when the car's not returned." She shook her head. "Any more new hires showing up at your office?"

"No. Thanks to you, the copycat took his show on the road." He shrugged, not wanting to think about that right now. Dinner with Melinda first and then meet Zeke at the office.

"That's good to hear. Things are going crazy at my office. I can't discuss that other situation with you. It's messed up, by the way. For some reason they thought I'd like lead on that case until I reminded them I still represented you on these other cases." She shook her head. "My days are numbered there for sure."

Uncertain what she needed or expected him to say, Leo covered her hand and squeezed. She smiled. The waiter returned with their salads.

"How are you holding up?" she asked after a few moments.

"Holding up?" He patted his lips with the linen napkin.

She leaned forward. "One of our clients informed the senior partner their group won the contract."

Leo stopped chewing, caught himself, and continued. "Really? How's that possible?"

She frowned. "It was announced last night. Didn't you know?"

"I found out this morning." *Thompson lied.* Why wasn't he surprised? "But I'm good. Hopefully now everything can return to normal."

"True." She stared at him for a few minutes. "You sure you're okay? That was a huge deal."

"One I never stood a chance winning."

Melinda frowned. "You don't know that."

He tilted his head and channeled his "get real" expression.

"You don't. Honestly, Leo, your program ... it's unbelievable. I hope you won't stop trying."

He snorted and continued eating. With someone asking about the creator of Venom, and the snake in his business, Leo didn't give two shits about government contracts. His priorities shifted to remaining out of jail and keeping his business afloat.

"Melinda." An older man graying at the temples with piercing gray eyes stopped at the table. Dressed immaculately in a charcoal gray suit, he outshined the gentleman standing next to him who wore similar apparel but lacked the stature or finesse of the first man.

She coughed and covered her mouth with her napkin as she looked up at him and then the person next to him. "Mr. Graves."

Leo glanced at both men and continued eating. He had no interest in speaking to one of the partners of the law firm who'd treated him so poorly.

After a few moments of silence, Melinda spoke. "Um ... excuse me, this is Leo Grit. Leo this is Mr. Graves, a senior partner of the law firm, and Mr. Wagram." Her voice wobbled initially, but strengthened by the end of the introduction.

Leo nodded at both men and promptly ignored them.

"Hello, Mr. Grit," Graves said, his voice smooth, like a seasoned social engineer. "If you have time I'd like to set up an appointment with you to discuss a few matters."

Leo met Melinda's surprised gaze. These assholes pissed on everybody. He placed his fork on the table and looked up at Wagram. "Let me guess, you're part of the group who won the contract?"

Wagram's eyes widened and then narrowed, but he didn't speak.

"Why do you ask that?" Graves asked, his gaze flicked to Melinda and then back to Leo.

"Just curious. I received a call that the bid has been awarded or will be before I hung up and since your prestigious company severed ties with me, I assumed it had something to do with the contract," Leo said, making things up as he went along.

"No, as Ms. Union explained there was a conflict of interest—"

"Ms. Union wasn't the one who told me services with your company had been severed. I received a letter by messenger informing me of the matter. I contacted her later for an explanation and that's when she explained the mistake."

"Yes. I see. We don't normally handle things in that manner," Graves said, glancing at Wagram and then back at Leo. "My apologies if it appeared abrupt or unprofessional. That wasn't the intent."

"Hmm …" Leo had no interest in a verbal smack down with this clown. They screwed him over and now expected him to play ball. Not happening.

"I'd like to set up an appointment to talk to you at your earliest convenience about a matter which could be very lucrative for you."

"No thank you," Leo said, picked up his fork and resumed eating.

"Have you talked to one of the others?" Wagram asked.

"I would never do business with a company who treated a paying client the way I was treated. You picked the wrong law firm," Leo told Wagram.

"What if Ms. Union handled the case?" Graves asked, his tone tense.

"No. Conflict of interest. Plus, she can't represent both sides," Leo said, enjoying Graves' discomfort. He looked at Wagram. "Get in touch with me and we'll talk."

"Excuse me." Melinda stood and left the table.

Wagram handed Leo his card and promised to be in touch. Leo noticed the man never asked for his phone number or office address.

Graves remained standing next to the table once Wagram walked off. "Was that necessary?"

Leo looked at the older man, slightly jealous of Graves' perfect tan this time of year. "Yes it was." He leaned back in his chair and waited.

"Because someone made a stupid mistake and cancelled your account? You're forcing Wagram to find new counsel just to deal with you?"

"I won't deal with your company ever again. Once Ms. Union finishes these last two cases for me, I'm done." Leo looked around the restaurant for Melinda, didn't see her, and returned to watching her boss.

Graves opened his mouth, closed it, nodded, and then walked away. Leo remained seated for a few minutes, wondering what happened to Melinda. He'd just asked the waiter for the check when she walked from the direction of the restrooms to the table.

When she sat, she grabbed her glass of water and took several large swallows. Chest heaving, she sat staring at the table for a few seconds.

"They want me to talk you into changing your mind about dealing with the firm. Obviously I'm supposed to use whatever it takes, including my womanly wiles, to convince you to forgive the massive insult, now called a mistake, and return to the lofty halls of billable hours." She'd spoken fast and then took a moment to inhale. Her slumped shoulders, refusal to look him in the eyes, and constant blinking pissed him off more.

Bullies.

He hated what they did to her. Whereas he hadn't wanted her to quit before, now he wanted her to march in her office, grab her things, and leave. *And then what?* His future wasn't very bright right now.

"I won't. Not even for you," he said, hoping she wouldn't be angry with him.

Her eyes flashed fire before they pinned him to his seat. "You'd better not or you're not the man I think you are. They're assholes. Smart assholes who made sure I couldn't sue their asses for this bullshit."

He covered her clenched fist.

"Sorry, I'm pissed … you have no idea how pissed I am, but I'm not getting disbarred behind this bullshit." She inhaled and smiled at him even though her eyes were hard as glass.

"Mr. Grit the firm of Miller, Brown, and Graves do apologize for the mix up concerning your account. Our company is built on a solid foundation of professionalism and good, quality service. If you'd be willing to overlook our tiny mistake, we'll handle your next cases without charge." She gave him two exaggerated Betty Boop eye blinks.

"Thank you, Ms. Union, but no thanks." Uncertain if she thought this was funny, a game, or just doing what she'd been told to do, he didn't like it. Not her words or the delivery. He pushed back, tossed a few bills on the table, turned and left. He pulled out his phone while waiting for the valet to bring his car around.

"Zeke?" he said when his friend answered. "How soon can you get to my office?"

Chapter 20

Wagram sat at the table with the other members of the consortium. Yesterday he'd gotten the news from the committee chair that they'd been awarded the contract. It'd cost more than their normal payouts for the committee to go against Thompson. In the end Thompson backed off for some reason and they made the award.

"We won the contract." He lifted his glass of bourbon in toast. Smothers and Gates raised theirs as well. They each took sips while looking at each other.

"Seems it cost more this year than before. Any problems?" Smothers asked, leaning back in his seat.

Wagram stared at the brown liquid in his glass for a few seconds. "Thompson wanted his new contractor to win, claims we need to keep up with the times." He tossed back the remaining contents.

"New contractor? Who?" Smothers asked.

"Keep up with the times? What did he mean by that? We provide cutting-edge services from the best companies in the country," Gates huffed. His hand shook slightly as he finished his drink.

"Cut the shit. We don't do this, not here, not now. We all have watchers, so you know about the company in North Carolina already." He slammed his glass on the table, drawing their attention. "We have a problem. Winning the contract didn't change that."

Smothers released a long sigh and ran his spotted hand through his thinning brown hair. "Leo Grit's firm has a remarkable response time. Thompson isolated and took out at least one target using that company. I noticed Grit ran into some problems, which is probably why he lost the contract, but if Thompson's coaching him that won't happen again."

"Plus his cost factor, he doesn't have a lot of staff, maintains the program himself and uses cell phones," Gates scoffed. "Bloody genius. I um ... I had a team try to replicate what he's doing."

"And?" Wagram asked when Gates remained silent. Had Gates found success where Wagram's hackers failed? Worse, had they heard the same rumors he'd heard about Grit?

Gates leaned forward. His pale blue eyes reflected the overhead light as he looked at his glass and then at Wagram and Smothers. "They could build a system that allowed uploads, that wasn't hard. Protecting that information?" He shook his head. "Not only could they not protect the data against threats, they couldn't hack into Grit's system. Even tried using images to access it and couldn't. That type of protection alone is worth millions."

"My team ran into the same problem. I think half of them would join Grit in a heartbeat if the guy wanted to expand. They offered to study the program on their own time to duplicate it." Smothers shook his head. "I don't know what to do about Grit, especially with Jackson and Thompson behind him."

"Jackson ... that's right he subcontracted with Grit in the bid. Now that's interesting," Wagram said, watching Gates. He'd used Jackson as a watcher before they started the consortium. "Have you talked to him lately, Jeff? What's his take in all this?"

"No, I haven't spoken to Jackson in years. Ask Fuller how Jackson's doing. I heard they have an unusual love-hate relationship, considering they were once partners during their military days." Gates looked at Wagram. "Jackson wouldn't toss water on me if I were on fire, let alone talk to me. If he's involved with Grit you can believe he's warned him about this group. If we want what Grit has, we'll need to handle him gently or not at all."

Wagram laughed.

Gates and Smothers looked at him.

"Gently? You think Grit is some gifted geek who requires Jackson and Thompson's protection?" He shook his head. "Leo Grit is the most dangerous man you've ever met. Don't think otherwise. If my information is correct, and drunk former roommates usually tell the truth, Grit's creation is responsible for the Leeks Financial job."

"What?" Gates straightened in his seat, leaning forward. "I lost everything in that deal. Everything about the company, even their charter was corrupted by a … a virus. It attacked my computer and everyone who'd ever logged into Leeks' system. It took months to stop it. Only half the accounts could be recreated because that damn virus searched everywhere and corrupted everything." His eyes looked haunted as he stared into his empty glass.

Smothers poured him another shot of Scotch and patted his back.

"Venom," Wagram said.

"What?" Gates asked after taking a hefty swig.

"The roommate called it Venom. Claimed no one's ever decoded or cracked it, whatever they call it." Wagram paused. "Sound familiar?"

Gates and Smothers nodded. No one spoke for a few moments.

"I don't see that we can do much here," Smothers said, glancing at Gates. "I remember the fallout from Leeks. It was bad. I don't want anything to do with Grit turning that thing loose on me or this group," he added hastily.

Gates continued staring at his glass. "At this point, Grit can't fulfill the contract, not the way it's written. I don't know why he bid. Thompson could've offered him a separate deal—"

"That's the question, isn't it?" Wagram asked watching his partners. "How much of our future contracts will companies like Grit's take?"

"None. He has no competition and Thompson will push that fact to use him. Right now, he's only in North Carolina. It takes time to expand, to build a network," Smothers said.

"So we sit back and allow him to grow, to take over? Is that what you're saying?" Wagram asked.

"I'm not sure that's the business I want to be in. Can I build a system to collect pictures and videos from the cell phones? Yes. Eventually my team will find a way to keep it safe, but what about long term? And at what cost?" Smothers asked.

"Thompson thinks it's worth something," Wagram said. "I'm going to open an office in Arizona, do a test run, and see if I can make it profitable."

"Hmm, not interested," Smothers said, turning up his nose. "I build equipment, not run spy offices."

Wagram shrugged. He didn't have the extra capital to compete against Grit right now and had hoped the consortium would pool their resources.

"Let us know how your experiment turns out," Gates said a few seconds later.

Smothers pointed at Wagram. "A copycat company? Sending people to his office? Shooting at his building? What if any of that's traced back to this group when you open a company?"

"That's down the road. No one will remember," Wagram said.

"Grit'll remember," Smothers snapped.

"Paying off the detective who worked for Grit was one thing, but Fuller crossed the line sending in the shooter. That might come back on us," Gates said.

"It won't. Fuller's been doing this a long time," Wagram said, adding confidence to words he didn't feel.

"That's before he stepped on Jackson's turf," Gates said, looking at Wagram. "Those two … you know things will get bloody when they're in the same state. Have you talked to your watcher lately?"

Chapter 21

Zeke found four bugs. Two in Leo's office. One in the conference room and one in the training room. The phone lines were clear, but Zeke bug proofed them anyway. He left a remote scanner in Leo's office that would flash pink when a listening device came in close proximity to his office.

Leo stared at the message that roused him from sleep and sent him back to his office an hour after he'd fallen into bed. The note from Thompson read *"Target en route. Flight arrives 0300 at private executive port."* Leo contacted Derrick and sent him to the airport to trail Blevins.

"Who's at the airport?" he murmured and clicked a few keys to see if anyone was in the area. He hit the jackpot. Two blue lights were at the smaller station.

Thompson wanted him at the airport, but he needed to get a good look at the target first. Mark, the skateboarder, worked at the jetport. Had Jackson planted Mark there this morning? Leo sent a message to both decoys.

"I need eyes and ears on an incoming flight."

Blue lights turned to green and flashed, signifying they received his instructions.

A few seconds later their apps activated and two live feeds filled separate monitors. Mark worked inside the terminal and talked to another worker. Cameron, the other decoy, worked outside in his position of security guard. Leo watched him walk around small jets, checking the area before sending more information regarding the flight and explained what he wanted.

"Eyes and ears on every person who deplanes. License plates when they leave, everything and anything."

Moving quickly, he left the room, grabbed a cup of coffee, and returned to his seat just as the plane taxied to a stop.

"I'm here," Derrick said. Leo received the visual of the airport. Few cars littered the lot.

"Good. I don't see his transportation but it should be there soon. Sorry, I don't have anyone to trade off with you. Keep your distance. I just need to know where he's headed tonight. I'll get more E&Es on it later."

"No worries. I've got this," Derrick said.

Tag and Craig worked the other job last night. According to Barb, the guys should be paying the company for all the action they received from the female target Thompson wanted occupied for a period of time. Consequently, none of his surveillance crew was available to assist on this job.

Cameron headed toward the small jet as it taxied to a stop and spoke casually to the two men headed toward the plane. The door opened and the ladder lowered. Cameron stood at the bottom and turned, looking at the three people leaving the plane.

He nodded and spoke. "Good evening."

"Hello," the first man said.

The other two ignored him and walked straight ahead into the terminal. Leo froze the picture of the man in the middle and verified it was their target. The live feed from Mark provided a better image.

None of the men spoke as they walked through the small waiting area outside. A dark S-Class Mercedes pulled along the curb when the jet touched ground. Mark stared into the security monitor, turned it slightly, and wrote down the license plate even though Leo saw it plainly on Derrick's camera as well.

"I'm with them. Wish we'd been able to tag that car," Derrick said.

"Yep, would've made things a lot easier," Leo agreed.

Outside, Cameron greeted the pilot and another male who may have worked on the flight. Leo took pictures of them all to run through the database.

"Stay with that plane, Cameron, in case someone gets off later or returns to remove something," Leo said.

Cameron's light flashed twice.

Inside Mark greeted the flight crew. It became obvious he'd seen them before. The captain returned his greeting and left. The host hung around the kiosk, talking to Mark. Leo turned up the volume and caught the tail end of a question.

"… on your board yesterday?" the guy asked.

"Yeah, every day after work and then I work here a few nights a week to pay for my boarding habit," Mark said.

"I heard that. Maybe I'll see you at Regal Park. It's sweet over there too."

"Regal Park?"

"Not too far from the mall."

"Yeah, yeah, I know it. That's far from campus, though. Chances are slim I'll board there, but thanks, Richard. Appreciate it."

"Here's my number, call and we can hang out over there sometime," Richard said.

Mark took it. "Thanks, man. You leaving town soon?"

"Not that I know of, but I'm on standby to work flights and can be called at any time." Richard looked around the small waiting room and then back at Mark. "Call me. Most of my jobs aren't as long or far as this one. Usually I'm back home after a few hours."

"Sounds good. Thanks, man. I'm always up for new places to ride my board."

Richard nodded and walked off. Mark moved to the security monitor and watched Richard walk across the parking lot and drive off.

Mark held the paper Richard gave him so that it was recorded.

Cameron recorded the plane being moved and parked. Soon after, he boarded the small plane, looked around, and then left. Thirty minutes later Mark signed off. Cameron would watch the plane to see if anyone returned or retrieved something from it for five more hours.

Leo cropped the faces of every person, ground workers included, for facial recognition searches through two national and one international database. Next, he ran the license plates for the Mercedes through the DMV. It belonged to a limousine service. No big surprise there.

Over the next hour he received information from the FBI's database, confirming the target, Oscar Blevins. The two men with him weren't yet identified. No hits on any of the workers, Richard, or the pilot.

"They turned into the Majesty Hotel. All three men exited the car and walked into the hotel. Should I follow them inside?" Derrick asked.

"Majesty Hotel," Leo murmured. Three blue dots. "Eyes and ears in the lobby, three men are checking in right now, can I get a visual?" He waited to see if anyone could reach the men before they slipped away upstairs.

Two of the blue dots moved in the same direction. "Come on, come on," he murmured, watching the clock.

"Go inside, Derrick. Verify target."

A few minutes later Derrick responded. "No one's here, the desk clerk said they've gone to their rooms already. She said there were three of them. Want me to try and access the hotel cameras to get a visual?" Derrick asked.

Leo stared at the front desk via his monitor. "No. Come back to the office. I need some help."

"Gotta get some gas, and grab a bite. Be there in an hour. That okay?" Derrick asked.

"Yeah, it's good."

Leo sorted through the files of the men accompanying Blevins on the flight. It had taken some digging, but he finally discovered their names and connections. Thompson hadn't sent much information, and a guy like Blevins had lots of practice shaking tails.

The man ate all kinds of food, didn't seem to prefer one over the other. Didn't socialize much. Leo continued staring at the page until the words merged. Shaking his head, he tossed aside the pages and went to grab a soft drink from the back.

"Man comes to town. No, a college town. What does he do? What does he want? Why not the Research Triangle? Raleigh or Charlotte if he's interested in weapons or information. Maybe he's going to talk with a researcher, chemist ..." He leaned against the counter and took another long pull of his drink.

"What's here that interests him? It's just a college town." He took another sip and froze. "Damn, what the hell's wrong with me?" Tossing the can into the trash he headed into his office and completed another search.

Blevins didn't have any kids, at least none he claimed publicly. But maybe ... for the next thirty minutes he searched, cross referenced, and continued digging until he found a possible connection.

"Yes!" Leo jumped up, smiling down at the picture on the screen. One of the men accompanying Blevins had a son enrolled in a high-ranking law school nearby. Richard Krenstizy.

Leo placed Richard's photo from the files and Blevins picture side by side. His grin widened. "Don't you two look nice together?" The familial resemblance was there in the eyes and nose. Why didn't Thompson tell him of the connection? If Leo found it in less than a day, they had to know, right?

He glanced at his watch, Derrick would be there soon. Leo accessed Richard's class schedule and personal information from the college. Scheduling decoys would be a lot easier now. He released a long breath, feeling the weight of the assignment lighten considerably.

The office door binged, signaling someone entered the front door. "Don't shoot, it's me," Derrick said.

"Come in here. You're still on the clock," Leo said.

Derrick walked in and looked at the monitor. "Who's this guy?"

"Mark captured his picture tonight. He was on the plane with the others dressed as a flight steward. I didn't pay him much attention then, but looking back maybe they planted a decoy of their own."

"Must be close then," Derrick said.

Staring at the monitor, Leo tapped his upper lip a few times, and then snapped his fingers. "Follow Richard."

"Huh?" Derrick stared at him

Leo met Derrick's gaze. "If we follow Richard, we'll find Blevins. Ten to one he's got someone masquerading as him at the hotel anyway. That car drove up just as they arrived. Someone could've been lying on the floor or backseat and changed places with Blevins."

"Good point," Derrick said. "What makes you think Blevins will go to the guy? Maybe we shouldn't focus on him alone and send eyes to watch the hotel."

Before Derrick finished, Leo shook his head and tapped his gut. "Instinct says he'll skip out on us and spend time with Richard."

Leo tapped the keys. A few seconds later the screen cleared. He typed more keys. A file downloaded, shapes sharpened into focus. Leo stared at Blevins in the middle. "He leaves the airport, but Richard hangs back. See how he's looking around, even though he's talking to Mark?"

"Umm hmm," Derrick said.

"I think he waited to make sure no one made a connection or followed the old man. They flew in together. There must be a reason Blevins is here and that young man is the key. I'm sure of it." Family, an Achilles heel for most and a blessing for his team.

"Okay, what do you need from me?" Derrick asked.

Leo searched Richard's neighborhood for the best place to run their operation. "We can mount a camera here. Just like the one you mounted when watching the doctor in the warehouse." Leo pointed to the roof of a townhouse for sale a few doors down, across the street from Richard's unit.

Derrick stared at the screen for a few moments and then nodded. "Shouldn't be a problem. I'll take the ladder from the back closet."

"Where can we mount another one to cover the back of his house? I'll even take a side … are you all home? Anybody out of town?" Leo murmured while looking at sales listings and a plat map of the street.

Leo pushed back from his desk and searched for the remote camera they used for these jobs. Derrick finished gathering his supplies to start surveillance and then strode down the hall toward the water cooler.

"Once it's in place, we'll run a test, make sure it's working, and then get some sleep. Start fresh in a few hours,"

Leo said as Derrick left the office with his bag in one hand and the ladder in the other.

"Sounds good."

Chapter 22

Derrick had gotten lucky. When he reached Richard's neighborhood, a house one street over had a 'For Sale by Owner' sign in the yard and was obviously empty. At 4:30 in the morning, few interior lights glowed. Derrick hadn't wasted any time installing both remote cameras on the two rooftops.

From the office Leo zoomed in on the target's home, granting visual access to both sides of Richard's house. Derrick attempted to get a heat signature reading to verify the number of people inside, but couldn't get an accurate accounting. They'd have to wait until Blevins or Richards left to positively identify both. Right now all they had was Leo's hunch.

Hours passed. With a large cup of steaming coffee, Leo sat in his car two blocks from Richard's house in the parking lot of a large chain drugstore. Every now and then a car would cruise close to his parked car, whether they noticed him staring at the screen displaying the target's location he didn't know.

All of his attention focused on this one hunch and the ramifications of him being wrong. Butterflies flitted in his gut as he went over this case in his mind and came to the same conclusion: Blevins had to be with Richard. For the sake of his career and company, he prayed this gamble paid off.

Derrick parked a few blocks in the opposite direction, both prepared to move whenever Blevins surfaced. Leo had given in to Barb's strong suggestions that someone cover the hotel as a precaution. She sat in a car nearby, waiting in case Blevins surfaced from the Majesty.

"A car is leaving the garage," Leo said, happy for signs of activity from the house. "He's headed in your direction."

"On it," Derrick said.

The townhouse had one garage. No cars lined the driveway. Uneasy over the tinted windows and inability to verify Blevins in the car, Leo continued watching the house.

"Turned onto the freeway headed toward I-40," Derrick said.

For someone who'd escaped detection for years, this seemed too easy. "Keep him in your sights. I've got a hunch they're still in the house."

"Hunch?" Derrick said. "Okay. I'll follow this one until you tell me different."

"Right." Five minutes later doubt seeped in eroding Leo's confidence. Maybe he made a mistake and Blevins was at the hotel. Or in the car Derrick followed.

Five minutes turned to ten.

Disappointed at the lack of activity and his wrong reading of the situation, Leo turned the key and started the car, prepared to catch up with Derrick before the car left the freeway.

A late model black Lexus pulled into Richard's driveway.

Leo leaned forward, staring at the screen. Blevins and Richard walked outside smiling and laughing before they entered the luxury car.

Heart racing, Leo copied the tag, and called it in to Craig.

"Got a visual, positive identification as they walked outside to get into another car. Target just left the driveway and is turning out the neighborhood." He manipulated the remote cameras to follow the car as far as possible.

"Seems headed in the opposite direction on Highway 147," Leo told Derrick as a rush of adrenaline flooded his system. Now they were getting somewhere.

"You pegged it. I'll get off the next exit and head toward you. I'm not that far," Derrick said.

Leo contacted Craig again. "Find out what's happening on Duke's campus today. Check the law school first, and if there's nothing happening, I want to know what's going on at Chapel Hill."

"Okay," Craig said.

From their vantage points, the cameras allowed Leo to watch the car until it reached the feeder road. He pulled out and followed. Minutes later he had the car in view and heaved a sigh of relief. Waiting to trail Blevins was risky, but if they were headed to one of the law schools they had time to set up a welcome. Leo could remain a good distance behind them until Derrick showed up.

"Mock trials on the Blue Devils campus. It's not the national competition, more like tryouts to be on the team. It's a big deal. Stacy, Denise, and a few of their friends are going. Nothing happening at Chapel Hill."

Leo released a long breath, grateful for the break. "Contact Stacy and Denise, eyes and ears only at the event. Have them mingle and capture as many faces as possible." He thought for a minute and called Craig again. "Anyone else on that campus?"

A few moments later Craig responded. "Twelve double E's, not including Denise and Stacy who aren't there yet."

Leo's brow rose at Craig's abbreviated term for eyes and ears. "Activate everyone. Eyes on a black Lexus with that license plate. I'd like eyes on the men who exit the car continuously. Then I'd like you to send live feeds to our monitors. I want everything recorded." That way he'd watch Blevins movements and anyone he talked to.

"Barb just called. Her target's on the move."

"Tell her to abort," Leo said, turning off the freeway.

"Abort?"

"Yes." Leo didn't explain.

"Will do. Stacy and Denise are excited and will let me know when they arrive. They'd taken today off, but now they'll be paid to watch the competition."

Leo didn't argue the differences between the job and the mock trials. Barb had shared Craig's interest in Stacy, which accounted for the green leprechaun sitting on the younger man's shoulder. "Turning off and heading toward the campus," Leo said as Blevins' car drove down the main road and then turned in the direction of the law school building.

Careful not to pass his target, Leo slowed to a crawl behind several others. His screen flickered, then cleared, showing the Lexus as it pulled to a stop.

"Yes!" Leo pumped his fist in the air. His face split into a wide grin as he parked in a remote lot and watched the monitor.

This is what he'd envisioned when he decided to embrace decoys: a large network of invisible eyes, decoys, operatives, whatever title applied for the job. Few people noticed college students using their phones, but there was a wealth of untapped information out there and his company specialized in harnessing that goldmine.

Blevins and Richard exited their car and moved with purpose toward the entrance. Leo had no idea which decoys captured the two or followed them inside.

"Great job, Craig, keep it coming."

"Denise and Stacy are heading inside now."

"Good. Is there anyone watching the car?

"Not really. I'll see whose outside."

"What's your ETA, Derrick?" Leo asked.

"Turning into the campus right now. You're in the parking lot near the field?"

"Yes. Park in the lot adjacent to the law school. We may need to move quickly."

"On it," Derrick said.

A visual of the Lexus split his screen. "Is the driver in the car?"

"I can't tell." The camera zoomed closer to the front, but he couldn't see through the darkened windows.

Leo studied the car for a few seconds. "Limousine service?"

"Yes, DMV records show Valley Limos owns that car," Craig said.

A visual of Blevins separating from Richard and moving into the stands before sitting on the last row in the back of the auditorium took up a large portion of the screen. The screen split with a visual on the Lexus and Blevins and Richard.

Derrick appeared on screen and walked behind the Lexus toward the school. He talked to a student who pointed across the street and then made gestures as if he was giving directions. Derrick nodded, headed in the direction the student gave, and disappeared. Minutes later an orange dot flashed on the screen.

"Good job," Leo said to Derrick. "Be interesting to see which way they go. I'm betting the airport. Do we have anyone working the jetport in Greensboro?" Leo asked Craig.

"I'm checking," Craig said.

"Check all the local ports. He could fly out of any of them," Leo said. "Heads up." The Lexus pulled out and another car pulled up. "They switched cars. Shit, that was my last tracker."

"Mark's working at the Greensboro jetport. Not sure about the old one at Chapel Hill. I think they closed it down," Craig said.

Leo wasn't sure either. "We'll wait and see which direction they go." For the next three hours, Leo and Derrick fought sleep while watching law students' debate.

Fascinating.

Leo's private cell beeped. He looked at the caller ID and frowned. "Thompson?"

"Just got a call from an acquaintance, Sam Fuller. He works for procurement, helps with investigations."

Leo tensed at the name and held the phone tight.

"According to Fuller, Blevins boarded a plane an hour and a half ago. He claims you've taken this agency for a financial joyride and never worked the case. Also suggested an inquiry into all the jobs you've done for us in the past. And it's not just me he's telling this. I just received a call from two high-ranking committee members. Interrupted my golf game. You may not have wanted the contract but this kind of thing, him talking to friends in high places, can make your life hell."

Leo stared at Blevins on the monitor and wondered if Thompson had contacted Jackson. Was this another bullshit game they played? When this job was over the three of them would talk, clear the air, or he wouldn't deal with any of them again.

"Fuller is full of shit, pun included. Blevins ditched him the first night at the hotel. He never stayed there. He has decoys of his own." Fuller had no idea how Leo's company actually operated, and because he couldn't fathom a group of independent civilians working for a common cause, he underestimated Leo's team.

"Make sure, your continued freedom rides on this."

"I trust my guys. Blevins never stayed at the hotel," Leo said with confident pride. "He's still in North Carolina."

"You've got eyes on him?" Thompson sounded relieved. It wasn't just Leo's reputation on the line.

"From the moment he walked off the plane." He stretched the truth just a bit.

Thompson released a breath. "Good, good, that's what I needed to hear to handle things on my end. I expect a report today."

"Will do, and pencil in a meeting with you, me, and Jackson when this is done." Leo's gaze never left the monitor as he disconnected. People clapped and stood. Richard left the stage and headed toward the side exit.

"Get me eyes outside that door now!" Leo told Craig.

Seconds later a visual of Richard smoking outside with two other guys flickered on the screen. Blevins hadn't moved from his seat but talked on his cell phone. Richard walked back inside and looked up at Blevins.

The two stared at each other for a few moments, nodded, and then Richard left the building. He and another student met outside and headed to the parking lot. Blevins walked with precise movements down the steps and then exited the building through the side door quickly to a parked, dark gray Cadillac. Once Blevins slid inside, it pulled out of the parking lot and passed directly in front of Leo.

"He's on the move," Leo said. He gave Derrick the color, make, and model of the car.

"Got him." Derrick pulled out right behind Blevins and gave Craig the license plate information. Leo peeled out in the opposite direction and took another route to enter the freeway below the Cadillac.

"They're heading to the jetport," Leo said after they merged onto the highway. "I'm turning off and will meet you there." He took the next exit.

Derrick remained a few cars behind Blevins and followed the car until it exited toward the same jetport Blevins arrived early this morning.

"Mark says a plane is waiting outside and these two men went onboard already," Craig said. The faces of the two men who arrived with Blevins flashed on the screen.

Leo placed a call to Thompson and with a few sentences brought him current.

"Did he talk to anyone?" Thompson asked, sounding relieved.

"Not at the event." Thompson's attitude surprised him. Leo expected shock, disappointment, anger. Instead, the old man accepted the abbreviated report and told him to send a full report when he returned to the office.

Leo turned in the opposite direction of the jetport. He parked at the nearby gas station and waited for Derrick.

"I've got him." Derrick said, seconds later. The Cadillac returned to the screen. The car stopped at the curb. Blevins exited the back seat, walked into the jetport, and looked at Mark.

"Good afternoon, sir. Can I help you?" Mark asked.

"No." He turned and headed to the plane.

Derrick walked into the small reception area as the plane taxied on to the runway.

Leo sat in his car, his fingers tapping the steering wheel as he watched the screen. "Has there been any activity on the house?" he asked Craig.

"House? The one from this morning?" Craig said.

"Yes. Has the young man returned home?"

"One second. Yes, he and a friend walked inside and are still there."

"Thanks," Leo said, his stomach jittery.

"The bird's in the air," Derrick said, pulling Leo's attention.

Leo placed a call to Jackson. "Guess who's in your backyard?"

Chapter 23

Elated from the successful completion of both assignments, Leo took the rest of the day off and came into the office early the next morning before anyone arrived. He nodded at Timms, who worked security at the front door, and headed toward the coffee station to make a pot. Soon his mouth watered as the aroma of ground coffee beans filled the air. He bit into the zucchini-nut muffin while eying the dark brew as it dripped into the pot.

Yesterday he redeemed himself, if not in the eyes of Thompson, definitely in his own. They'd finished the job in less than twenty-four hours and made a lot of money. Thompson had been pleased with the results and the report. Leo gave himself a mental fist bump.

Taking a large mug he filled it to the brim, sipped and moaned as warmth spread through him. Stoked, he'd pulled out his phone to call Melinda to celebrate, momentarily forgetting their last meeting and the earliness of the hour. His finger hovered over the send button and he canceled. No need to make a nuisance of himself. She hadn't answered or returned any of his calls since that night in the restaurant.

He glanced at his phone and then headed to the console. A few seconds later he zeroed in on her blue dot, she was home. For some reason that made him feel better. Should he call? They were friends if not the lovers he'd hoped they'd become. What would he say? That he missed her? Should he apologize for being rude to her boss? Ask if he made things difficult for her at work?

Leo rubbed the back of his neck and shoved his phone into his pocket. Out of habit, he initiated a deep scan of the system, took another look at her blue dot on the monitor and headed to his office. Maybe he'd call her later.

He booted up his computer and then checked the security cameras on the building from last night. One of the tenants on the first floor worked late. A couple cars were parked in the lot, but other than that nothing out of the ordinary.

What happened to the copycat company, he wondered and ran a search throughout the state to see if they competed against him in other areas. When he saw no signs of activity, he sent emails to several decoys in Raleigh, Charlotte, and Ashville, asking if they'd heard anything about the company. Regardless of his thoughts on healthy competition, he preferred to know if and when that happened rather than be taken by surprise again. No one had heard anything.

Wagram had called to set up a meeting, but Leo had taken yesterday off to rest from the last job and hadn't talked to the man. If he wasn't curious to hear the sales pitch from the consortium, he wouldn't entertain a meeting with the guy. But it fed his bruised ego that they courted his business and he planned to hear them out when he had time.

Cherise left a message that two men, Gates and Smothers, called while he was at the college watching Blevins. They wanted to speak with him but left no message. Leo recognized their names from the list Jackson gave him. Melinda had been right about the men who won the contract wanting to talk to him.

He pulled up the files he'd created on Wagram, Smothers, and Gates. Of the three, Wagram was the youngest with impressive credentials from Harvard. He married a woman three years older from old money and they had two kids in high school. Leo stared at Wagram's picture for a few moments. There were a lot of them scattered over the internet. Something about the man's eyes didn't sit well with

Leo. This wasn't a man you turned your back on or shared a cup of coffee with. Leo planned to avoid meeting alone with Wagram, maybe he'd talk Jackson into sitting in the conference call.

He read the information on Smothers, the oldest of the trio, and then Gates. These two men had made and lost fortunes over the years and were probably ready for retirement. Leo's gaze returned to Wagram and his young kids. This man couldn't retire, not yet. He'd need the contracts to maintain his lifestyle and expensive wife. Wagram would be the one to watch, and then Gates. Leo dug deeper into Wagram and Gates' life, searching government and social media databases for hits. Next he entered their addresses in the mapping program and pictures of their homes appeared. It didn't take much to access Wagram's household account to learn who handled his cleaning and maintenance services. Staring at the information, he debated the merits of being proactive or waiting to see what happened when he refused to sell. Rather than make a decision, he downloaded the information on all three men to files and sealed them.

Thoughts of protecting his company filled his mind. Men like Wagram did their dirty deeds in the shadows while smiling in the light. Maybe Leo could copy them this time. Set up cameras in places Wagram and the others felt safe, gather information that would keep them at a distance.

Massaging his forehead, he went for another cup of coffee and returned to the console room to run additional system checks since the scan returned clean. His phone chirped. He looked at the caller ID. Carter.

"Hello?" Leo leaned back in his chair and took a sip of coffee.

"I need to talk to you," Carter said, the voice held a ring of urgency.

"No can do, you're suing me, remember?"

"I never said that. Well, I said it but didn't mean it. Look, those tapes you have of my wife at the club, do you still have them?"

Leo leaned forward. Detective Bronson never explained the connection, if any, between Leo's company and the murdered girl. "Why?"

"Stop." He paused. "Just answer me. Do you have them?"

"Yes."

"Destroy them. I'll pay you anything you want if you wipe the slate clean of what happened that night." An underlying thread of desperation rang through his voice.

"Sorry, I can't do that," Leo said, no longer enjoying the conversation.

"Why not? I paid you. Technically that information belongs to me," he said.

"No, read your contract. I gave you your copy, but I keep copies on file for five years as an added layer of protection. I can't help you."

"Wait," Carter yelled.

Leo rubbed his forehead. This was not a part of the morning he expected. "What?"

"Have the police been there? Have they asked about the pictures of my wife?"

"Yes."

"Shit. Shit. Shit. Okay ... okay they know she was with that ... with Drake, but that's all it was, harmless fun between girls, you understand."

"Yes, Mr. Carter, I do. Have a good day, I have another call." He hung up and closed his eyes for a moment. Carter, man or woman, was falling apart. From what Jackson told him, Graham hadn't been charged with anything. The jewels hadn't been found and witnesses saw him at the strip club.

Carter, on the other hand, was the lead suspect in Drake's murder.

Leo stared at the phone for a few seconds and then placed another call. Detective Bronson answered on the third ring.

"Morning, Detective, this is Leo Grit, do you have a minute?"

"As long as it's a minute."

"Is there any connection between my company and the murder investigation? What I mean is, have you cleared me and my employees from whatever you needed from us?"

"Griff tried to leave town."

Leo's jaw tightened. "Yes, after I fired him I realized someone may have paid him to ruin that job for me." But the older man hadn't gotten far, Leo made sure of that.

"Because of that contract?"

"Yes. Seems I have a lot to learn when it comes to bidding on high dollar jobs."

"Jackson can help you with that. I can't discuss the case with you, but I can say as of right now your company is not involved. In fact, I've suggested strongly to the chief that we implement a similar system to gain assistance from the public."

Leo cringed at another copycat trying to implement his idea. "That's great, I wish you the best with that."

"Yeah, he liked the idea but isn't sure how it would pan out. He had a lot of questions I couldn't answer. He said he'd pitch it to IT."

"Awesome. Thanks for answering my questions. I won't hold you." Leo had no intention of offering any type of consults and wanted to disconnect the call before the detective ventured down that road.

"No problem, take care," Bronson said.

Leo exhaled, glad they were removed from that tangle. He glanced at the security cam and saw Jackson drive up. Anxious to hear what happened between Fuller and Jackson, Leo went to refill his cup of coffee. He met Jackson in the reception area.

Except Jackson wasn't alone.

Thompson stood next to him, looking around. Leo wondered if they were looking for the bugs he'd had removed.

"Morning. This is a surprise," Leo said.

Jackson chuckled. "No it's not, you saw us arrive."

Leo tilted his head to the side and took a sip of his brew. "Coffee?"

"Yes, I'd like a cup," Jackson said and headed to the back. "Want one Barnaby?"

"No, promised the wife I'd cut back and I've already had a cup this morning." He watched Leo for a few seconds. "Is there someplace we can all talk? I think it's time."

"Past time," Leo murmured as he waved him toward the conference room.

He waited for Jackson and walked in last. He glanced at the detector Zeke left. It hadn't changed colors yet so his office should be free of listening devices. Taking a seat across from both men, Leo set his cup down and waited.

"First off, congratulations on a job well done. It bears repeating, we didn't know about the college student Blevins visited and doubtful we would've thought of that angle since there's no record of the kid anywhere. Blevins has gone underground again, which we expected. We had no legal grounds to arrest or hold the man."

Leo's brow rose as he recalled the incident in the parking lot of the club and wondered if Blevins met a similar fate. He looked at Jackson, who stared into his cup of coffee, the skin broken and cut on his knuckles in places. Was that a bruise on his chest just behind the buttons on his shirt? What the hell happened?

Thompson hesitated for a few seconds, leaned forward, and spoke into the silence. "The committee was interested in this case, more importantly on how your company handled the case. Ever since you submitted your bid using a network of civilians and cutting edge technology, it's been discussed by those with the power to make something like this happen on a wide scale."

Leo glanced at Jackson. His throat tightened at the mention of the committee. He didn't relish the idea of being beneath their microscope, not with Venom's name on a few lips.

"Yet they awarded the bid to the consortium," Jackson said dryly.

Yep, definitely a bruise on the chest. Leo saw it clearly when Jackson moved. *Fuller?*

"That happened before this last test," Thompson said.

"How many tests did they need to see this is the wave of the future?" Jackson asked.

Leo had the feeling this conversation had been a running dialog between these two.

"Doesn't matter, they see it now." Thompson turned to Leo. "They want you to recreate what you have here in other cities. Once you cover a larger area, they'd like to see the results."

"It's taken me three … well … five years to get this far," Leo said, his tone wary.

"I'm aware of that. You worked most of the bugs out of the system, which means you could duplicate your efforts in a larger or smaller area faster," Thompson said.

Leo looked at Jackson. "What about the bastards out to shut me down?" If Jackson forgot the gloomy predictions from their last conversation, Leo hadn't.

"They'll still try but you've got something they haven't been able to duplicate," Jackson said softly.

Ice-cold dread rolled down Leo's back. How did Jackson know? "Really?"

"Yes. You've worked on it since what? High School? College?" Jackson asked while Thompson sat back and watched.

"Not sure what you're talking about." Leo met Jackson's gaze without flinching. Revealing Venom wasn't an option, and he refused to share Ghost with anyone.

Jackson leaned forward and smiled. "You created a virus that eats data, changes and then regurgitates it, and then eats it and corrupts all data connected to that system like a snake. It can move through a system slowly, almost undetectable, or zip through, leaving nothing behind. No one's been able to break it. No one knew who created the virus but it has your fingerprints all over it."

Leo smiled, showing few teeth. "I'll take credit for it if that'll move this discussion along."

Jackson's smile slipped a fraction. "You created it. I have someone who swears you did it."

Leo shrugged, wondering how soon he could kick Zeke's ass. "I already took credit, what else do you want me to do?"

Jackson stopped smiling and stared at him. "What about Ghost? Is that something else you created? Is that the reason it's impossible to hack into your system and access your program?"

Leo leaned back in his chair, stared at Jackson, and then laughed. "So you've been trying to hack into my system too? Not surprised." He looked at Thompson. "You wanted him to replicate what I was doing? That's why he sent decoys to work for me? When I opened the system the other day to track Delgado, someone tried to infiltrate my system. Did they work for you?" he looked at Thompson and then Jackson. "Or you?"

"Me," Jackson admitted. "I was asked to learn how you were able to do what you do. On the surface it seems easy. When I couldn't crack it, I told Thompson to hire you. But the challenge of hacking into your system was too tempting to pass up. You're one bad hombre." Jackson leaned forward with his fist held out to Leo.

Leo bumped it. At least Jackson manned up to what he'd done. "What does any of this have to do with the men who won the contract?"

"Chances are they are all discovering what Jackson and I have. It's almost impossible to recreate what you've done in a cost effective manner. Believe me, I've tried and had the best hackers from the cave work on it for over a year. The fact the data is impenetrable so far makes it perfect for the kind of jobs we need done," Thompson said.

"Wagram's been calling, so have two of the others." He couldn't remember their names. "I'm not selling my program or business, and I will protect it."

"Like you took care of Delgado and his family? Seriously, you turned the IRS onto them for cleaning Delgado's money? I know one warrant has already been issued for the ex-wife and Delgado for tax evasion. Strange, the IRS doesn't normally move that fast. They jumped right on this case. Was it something you said?" Jackson asked with a chuckle.

Thompson smiled.

Leo's cheeks warmed. "It was the IRS or the DEA."

"Ouch," Jackson said. "You are mean. Griff sold you out and thought he'd get to take the money and run. Heard all of his assets are frozen. Seems there's some confusion as to who he is, one of the worst cases of identity theft I've ever seen. Poor man can't access any money, his DMV records vanished so he can't drive, and none of his credit cards work." Jackson tsked.

Griff had been arrested once he crossed the state line for grand theft and a bench warrant for failing to appear in court for an older case. Pity the money he'd received for botching the insurance job was unavailable.

Leo shook his head without comment.

"About expanding," Thompson said.

"I told you I planned to expand, first in Virginia and then South Carolina," Leo said.

"Yes, yes you did. You also promised to be available for use. Which means more surveillance and decoy workers," Thompson said.

"I'm aware of that," Leo looked at Jackson, wondering where all of this was going.

"This will be your own company with various offices in key locations, not an extension of my department. There are times we'd hire your services, but you'd own it completely," Thompson stressed, his gaze latching onto Leo's.

"Some cases I may not want after I complete my research. With all our clients there's a twenty-four hour window where the contract can be terminated. Can you work with that?"

Thompson's jaw tightened. He tapped his fingertips on the table for a few seconds. "Sometimes … sometimes I can't stop a job. I couldn't allow you to cancel that last job."

"Because Blevins is someone you've wanted a long time? How does that work if you let him go underground again?" Leo asked, allowing his skepticism to come through.

"Blevins is important. Another agency is handling him now. We did our part, but … I wanted them to see how well your organization worked. How quickly you mobilized. We need to change with the times and operate more efficiently."

His gaze remained on the table, missing Jackson's raised brow.

"Budgets ... every department jockeys for more and more money, each claiming they have the greatest need." Thompson's hands were in motion, waving about to emphasize his points until he clasped them together and dragged them onto the table.

"The committee has limited access to what it's like to run an operation these days and depends on doctored reports and whoever is their flavor of the day to make decisions. To be effective, we need to move with the times and technology. Five years ago you had an idea, it had potential, but it was weak in its infancy form, lots of potholes. But you've fixed those and created an excellent, vibrant network, one I wanted to include in my budget for bigger jobs."

Leo frowned. He'd lost the contract and was okay with that.

"To do that I needed something that would get their attention. Fuller ran true to form and provided the opening. Your team performed seamlessly with no casualties in a timely matter. The committee was suitably impressed."

"Your budget was approved?" Leo asked trying to follow the conversation.

"Yes and enlarged to handle domestic cases," Thompson said, his eyes alit with fire. "That's why I'd like you to consider expanding your company to other key cities. If we could prevent some of the senseless killings or discover the perpetrators and victims as quickly as you found Delgado ... that could turn the tide in our favor of stopping domestic terrorists."

Domestic terrorists?

Leo's heart raced. So far they'd handled cases where a decoy held the attention of a target while taping a conversation or while someone else searched a room or something. Or they trailed a target like Blevins. He'd never thought in terms of terrorism and wasn't sure he wanted to be associated with Thompson's program.

"Most decoys are college students," Leo said, his tone low. The weight of what Thompson wanted knocked the wind out of him.

"Exactly. Smart, energetic, and flexible, our country's future. Pay them well and on time and you have a loyal group ready to let you see the world through their eyes. You proved that formula works."

Leo opened his mouth and then closed it.

Thompson continued. "They don't know or care why they turn on their cameras. Most of them record everything they see anyway and throw it on the internet. But you've connected those visuals into a powerful tool, a sea of eyes and ears. No one person tells the whole story. If one person doesn't show up, there are several others ready to step into the gap." Thompson's gaze flicked from Leo to Jackson. "The ultimate network, that's what you've created."

Leo cleared his throat. "I'll keep you informed of my expansion, just keep sending us jobs."

Thompson nodded and slid a flash drive across the table. "I've got plenty for you and Jackson to handle. Here are my suggestions for possible cities to expand. Also, my budget increased for recruitment of any outstanding decoys you've trained, and consulting fees."

Leo stared at the flash drive for a few seconds and then took it. "So the Blevins job was a test?" He shouldn't be surprised, but he was. Thompson turned out to be a sneaky bastard.

"Partially." Thompson leaned back in his seat. "I had a snake too close to my department I needed to get rid of as well." He held up his hand and shook his head. "No questions about that, just know this, Fuller doesn't work for government procurement anymore."

Leo smiled before glancing at Jackson. "Well, that's good news."

Jackson didn't meet his gaze.

"One question," Leo asked as more things fell into place.

"Alright," Thompson said.

"That whole bidding thing, I never stood a chance, right? You did all of that to get rid of Fuller?"

"I knew you couldn't win the bid. Jackson was in place to watch out for you, and I picked up the tab for most of it. That whole ordeal exposed more than Fuller's corruption of leaking information, taking bribes, and extortion. It also highlighted those on the committee who were for sale. They've been replaced as well as a large portion of the procurement officers. Big shakedown that was long overdue."

Thompson nodded, stood, and extended his hand. Leo shook it and walked him to the door. Craig and Cherise entered as they reached the exit.

"Morning," Craig said, looking Thompson over.

Cherise waved and left them standing near the exit as she went into her cubicle.

"Morning," Thompson said, nodding. He glanced at Leo and Jackson. "Hope to hear from you soon."

Leo nodded.

Jackson stood in the conference room door, watching. They waited until Thompson entered the elevator and then stared at each other.

"What the fuck just happened?" Leo asked, not quite sure what he thought happened really happened.

"You got your contract," Jackson said, his smile reaching his eyes. "Not the one you bid on, this one's open ended for sole sources, companies who provide one-of-a-kind service. Much better deal, trust me. At least until someone copies what you're doing and competes against you."

"Dude ... seriously?" Leo's face warmed with an inner light. He couldn't remember ever smiling this wide.

Jackson nodded.

"Fucking awesome!" Leo said as the grin enveloped his whole body, lifting him higher than he'd been in years.

All his work and sacrifice finally paid off. Thompson basically offered carte blanche to underwrite the expansion of their operations. He pulled the flash drive from his pocket and stared at it for a few seconds as if it held the secrets of the universe.

"Everything alright?" Cherise asked, walking toward them.

"Everything's great!" Leo said, running to the back.

Laughing, Jackson turned and followed. "We have to talk."

Chapter 24

Melinda looked at the papers on her desk and then stared out the window behind her desk. For twenty years she'd wanted to be an attorney. As a teenager she'd watched *Perry Mason*, *Matlock* and every *CSI* episode imaginable, always wondering how she'd handle the cases when they went to court.

Back then she never lost a case.

As the only daughter to blue-collar workers, her parents assumed her two younger brothers would succeed in sports and placed their hard-earned dollars to make those dreams a reality. Melinda scraped and struggled with financial aid and student loans until she made it to law school. Working hard was all she knew. It didn't bother her in the least as long as she was on track to fulfill her dream of being the next *Perry Mason*.

But that was fifty minutes of fantasy.

Melinda had warned Leo about the sharks who'd come after him once he entered his bid, but hadn't realized how his bid would impact her future. The window reflected a whispery image of her face, making her appear shallow with limited substance. Her throat tightened in recollection of her last conversation with Leo in the restaurant. Bastard tossed a junior partnership in front of her as if she had no fucking moral compass if she'd talk Leo into signing with them. Worse, she'd agreed to do it. She closed her eyes and pressed two fingers against the bridge of her nose.

"You sold yourself, told everything you knew about him," she murmured in disgust. "They're circling like sharks smelling blood, looking for an opening."

Her assistant tapped on the door and stuck her head inside. "Don't forget you have a meeting in the conference room in five minutes. Mr. Graves called personally to remind me to remind you."

Melinda forced a smile and swallowed hard. This was what it all came down to, being a team player. Making decisions that would impact the rest of your life. She closed her eyes and saw Leo's smile across the dinner table, his face filled with pride as he showed off his system, his face meeting hers when he kissed her that night. Her fingertips brushed against her lips. The knock tapped again, pulling her out of her musings. She stood, grabbed a note pad, her tablet, and stuck her cell phone in her pants pocket. With one last look out the window, she inhaled and headed to the conference room.

Graves and Wagram sat at the table along with another man with bruises all over his face. A thick bandage covered his left hand. It was apparent he was in pain. She closed the door and took a seat.

"Wagram you've met our bright star, Melinda Union," Mr. Graves said, smiling at her as he stood.

Wagram and the other man remained seated. Mr. Graves frowned, presumably at their lack of manners.

"Yes I have," Wagram said, his dark green eyes met hers. He waved toward the other man. "Fuller, a business associate."

Melinda nodded and pulled out her chair.

"Has any progress been made with Leo Grit?" Wagram asked before she took her seat.

Graves cleared his throat. "He has not agreed to meet with us."

"I thought you had an inside track with this attorney. They were eating a meal when we stumbled on them the other day," Wagram said, his tone combative.

"I never said we had an inside track," Graves said in a cool tone. "We've asked him to meet with us on several occasions, he chose not to. I told you this."

Wagram waved away Graves comment. "I know, but I wanted to talk with Ms. Union and this was the only way that could happen." He turned toward Melinda. "According to Graves here, you've seen this system Grit uses to handle his operation. Is it all in one room? Are there a lot of computers? Monitors? How exactly does it work? How does he keep up with all those people?"

Her eyes widened beneath the barrage of questions. Fuller's gaze never left her face. "When Mr. Grit showed me his system, he specifically said it was to assist me in defending him against a copycat company. Anything I saw or heard is completely confidential." She fingered her phone, wishing she could record this meeting. Turning, she leaned on the table and pulled out her phone, resting it on her leg.

"Don't give me that, he's not a client of this firm—"

Her phone beeped. "One second let me put it on vibrate." She pulled it out, tapped a few keys while putting it on vibrate and returned it to her pocket.

"So if you severed your relationship with Jackson, Brown, and Graves it would be alright to discuss your private matters with other people?" she asked.

"Ms. Union," Mr. Graves said.

Wagram smiled and leaned forward. "It's a valid point and had you revealed anything he said to you in confidence, I would sever my relationship with this firm and turn you into the bar. You'd no longer practice law, no one would hire you, not even as a secretary bringing her boss a cup of coffee. So do not play with me."

"There's no need to become hostile," Graves said, looking from Wagram to Melinda. "Ms. Union is here to assist on this case. If she can share information, she will."

Melinda's face burned, but she remained silent.

"What do you know about Venom?" Wagram asked.

She frowned. "What?"

"A virus your former client created," Wagram said, watching her closely.

She shook her head. "Nothing. I never heard of it until now."

Wagram nodded. "Ghost. Has he ever mentioned Ghost to you?"

She frowned and shook her head. "No, never heard that before either." Obviously Leo hadn't told her much, and she was glad he hadn't.

Mr. Graves' secretary tapped on the door. He stood and peeked out. They talked briefly, and she handed him a cell phone. "Excuse me one second." He stepped outside the room but remained on the other side of the door, talking.

Melinda sensed that had been pre-planned and wondered why she remained in their employ. None of them had a shred of decency and would gladly toss her beneath the bus to make a dollar.

"What would it cost to receive photos of Grit's system?" Wagram asked as soon as the door clicked shut. "I'd pay you a staggering amount for pictures or if you can get any information regarding Venom or Ghost. You'd be set for life and can open your own firm."

She jerked and met Wagram's steady gaze. The man just admitted he'd ruin her if she lacked morals and then made that offer?

"I can't. He's not talking to me, doesn't trust me. I've only been in his control room once and that was to show me the system so I could defend against the copycat."

"It's massive, fast, cutting edge that's for sure," Wagram said, leaning back. "Does he intend to expand? Work in more states?"

"He didn't say, but I believe he may," she said, meeting Fuller's glossy-eyed gaze. "Excuse me, are you alright?" she asked, looking at him.

Fuller's face reddened as he sat back. "I'm good."

Her brow rose in the face of such a blatant lie.

"Where would Grit expand first? Any ideas?" Wagram asked, his elbow on the table leaning forward.

"He never discussed any of that with me. I handled the case I mentioned and no more."

The door opened and Graves stepped back inside.

"Thank you very much, Ms. Union, you've been very helpful," Wagram said, smiling. "We'll be in touch."

"Sorry I couldn't be of more help," she said surprised by the change in his voice and behavior.

"Oh, you've helped more than you know. We appreciate it and promise to take care of you and the company." Wagram stood and slapped a frowning Graves on his back.

Uncertain what was going on, but ready to leave the room, Melinda stood and looked at Mr. Graves, who appeared as confused as she did. "If that's all?"

Graves looked at Wagram. "Do you need anything else?"

"No, I'm good." He waved to Fuller, who stood slowly. "We appreciate your time and trust. Have a great day." Wagram slapped Graves on the shoulder again as he walked out without a backward glance at her.

Chapter 25

Jackson closed the door behind him as he entered Leo's office. The morning had a few bumps but turned out stellar. Leo couldn't stop smiling.

"I need to explain a few things so you don't think I'm some kind of douche," Jackson said, taking the seat in front of Leo's desk.

Leo sat in the chair next to it rather than behind his desk. "Okay."

"Like I said, I heard about your company through Mark, but didn't trust it. The whole concept is too fucking simple and I saw potholes everywhere. I never thought you could pull it off and was sure it was a scam."

During Jackson comments, Leo's grip tightened around the coffee cup while he forced his face to remain neutral. "That's damn insulting," he said when Jackson finished. "Why didn't you simply come by and talk?"

Jackson snorted. "Too busy. In and out of town a lot back then, but I promised Thompson I'd keep an eye on you."

"But you made time to try to break into my system."

Jackson nodded. His face sobered. "I thought this was a scam taking advantage of college students. I also encouraged Thompson to hire hackers which he did."

"Did you bug my place as well?"

Jackson nodded. "I had a bug placed in your office, yes. You removed them."

"Them?"

"Yes. We were afraid you might betray secrets," Jackson said, crossing his knee and meeting Leo's gaze.

"Do you have any idea how offensive that is?" Leo asked, unsure how to process such blatant honesty.

Jackson sighed. "The contract Thompson extended to you was to me as well. There are things your company isn't equipped to handle that will fall to me. I assumed you wanted the air clear between us, so I'm coming clean."

"You can't expect me to trust you?" Leo asked, turning in his seat to try and read the man.

Jackson shrugged. "That's on you, although I've never lied or misled you. But..." he pointed a finger at Leo "...when it comes to work, we'll be honest and upfront. I won't ask how you created your program, or about Venom. I understand the risks of coming clean about that, but I will want to know what you can do on a job. I'll trust you to tell me any limitations truthfully so we can finish assignments."

Leo frowned at the mention of Venom and wondered how much Jackson knew. The man seemed certain of his information but Leo couldn't risk asking questions. "Why are we working together now? What's changed?" He didn't hear Thompson mention anything about them working together.

"Every job you've done for Thompson, my team worked the other side. The club, the hotel, the airport, we've worked together for all the jobs so far. We make a good team and he's not changing that." He paused. "So my question is this, knowing what you know, can you work with me or not?"

"Am I supposed to believe you trust me now?" Leo asked, leaning back in his chair.

"Professionally, yes. I trust your ethics and capability to get the job done under pressure."

Tension rolled off Leo's back with Jackson's answer. Pleasure blossomed in his chest that someone with Jackson's background believed in him and his company. There'd been many days he doubted their ability to cross the finish line, so a little praise eased his spirit.

"How will that work? Will we both get the entire job and split it? Or will Thompson split the jobs and send them like he's done in the past?" Leo asked.

"No. We'll get the entire order, put our heads together, and strategize the best way to complete the assignment. Unless you rather not know …"

"I don't." He paused at Jackson's frown. "Not initially anyway while I work on expanding. I've got a lot on my plate."

"Thompson's not going to continue splitting our assignments. His department just expanded. How do you want this to happen?" Jackson pinned Leo with his gaze, allowing him no room to back out or ignore his responsibility. "You want the work, it comes with a price, planning and strategizing. I'm not going to do it all."

Leo swallowed hard under the realization he had a partner of sorts who he didn't fully trust. Then again, who did he fully trust? *No one.* Time to make some changes.

"Okay, after we read the assignments we'll split the work. But if he has something only your company can do, I don't want to know about those. Thompson should send those to you alone, right?"

Jackson stood. "That's how it's done. You've got heart. I like that."

Leo accepted the compliment with a nod, liking Jackson's forthright manner. "You mentioned Griff. Was he the snake in my office?"

"Yes, Fuller paid him off to slack on the job. Wasn't hard, Griff wanted to leave here for a while. The money from Fuller made it possible to leave sooner. If it helps, he had a Judas moment afterward, wished he hadn't done it."

Leo snorted and wondered if he should ask who told him about Venom but left it alone.

"Did Griff bug my office? Is that how Fuller found out what happened with the insurance company?"

Jackson nodded. "Yeah. I tracked Griff after agreeing to partner with you, heard his conversations with Fuller." He looked at his skinned knuckles. "It was hard waiting for Thompson to give me the go ahead to deal with Fuller, but he needed the man to run his mouth, overplay his hand first."

Leo marveled at Jackson's calm and hoped he'd never become that unaffected by all the things Fuller had done. "Overplay his hand, that's one way of looking at it," he said and left the office.

Chapter 26

"I'm on my way," Leo hung up the phone and then stuffed his phone in his pocket.

After meeting with Thompson this morning and Jackson later, he was ready to meet Tag, Craig, and Derrick at a local bar near campus. Things were looking up for his business if not his personal life. Melinda still wouldn't talk to him.

Jackson insisted he continued with security at the business and his home. Timms drove him to the bar and let him out in front.

"I'm not sure how this works. I just call you when I'm done or have one of the guys drop me off at home?" Leo said.

"I'm going to park and come inside," Timms said and then pulled off from the curb.

Derrick opened the door of the bar and waved. "Glad you made it. Come on, everybody's here."

Glad to see his friend and excited about sharing the good news about the company, Leo took two steps and spun around. A gunshot, the sound too powerful to be a backfiring car, reverberated in air. Something hot and heavy pierced his left shoulder sending him to the ground.

"Get down!" someone yelled.

"Oh shit," Derrick screamed.

Footsteps ran around Leo's head as excruciating pain so sharp his mind could barely comprehend the burning deep in his shoulder as if the bone smoldered. Tormented, unable to form complete sentences, his words reduced to incomprehensible snippets of pitiful moans and whimpers, a new vocabulary created out of a haze of agony.

"Stay with him," Timms yelled, his voice came from a distance.

"Fuck man, are you okay?" Derrick asked.

Leo opened his eyes and tried to smile but doubted he was successful. "Fucking fantastic."

Derrick's eyes widened and then he shook his head. "Yeah, stupid question."

Craig and Tag surrounded Leo.

"What the fuck happened?" Tag demanded.

"He was walking inside and somebody shot him," Derrick explained.

"Don't move him," Craig said. "He could have spinal damage."

"The bullet went into his shoulder," Derrick said.

Sirens blared in the distance.

"Bout time they got here. I called them as soon as he fell," Derrick said.

"Who's riding with him?" Craig asked.

"Does it matter?" Tag said. "I swear the things you think about ..."

"Leo? The paramedics are on the way, hang in there. They'll be here soon," Derrick said, laying his hand on Leo's hand.

"What happened? That's a lot of blood." Voices blended together, asking questions, and he had no answers.

"Who's that?"

"Somebody shot him? Here? In the open?"

Leo shut out the sounds around him as the throbbing pain in his shoulder spread through his body.

"Hold on, the paramedics are here," Tag said.

For the next few minutes someone asked questions he struggled to answer. He was lifted and taken away.

Jackson strode through the hospital doors and met Timms in the emergency room. "You get a look at who did this?"

"Not a good look, but I saw him running. It wasn't Fuller, somebody younger, college or high school student. Gray hoodie, jeans, red sneakers, short, medium build." He released a long breath. "Happened fast. I saw him go down in the rear view mirror, jumped out, and ran after the guy."

Jackson placed his hand on Timms shoulder. "Thanks. Heard anything so far?"

"Not yet, but I saw him on the ground. The bullet ripped through his shoulder. Might have gone clear through."

"I contacted Bronson, not sure what he can do, but if there are any cams in that area I'd like to look at it." He stared at Timms who nodded and left.

Jackson read his text messages as he headed into the emergency waiting room area to find Leo's friends. Three of them surrounded the nurse station and turned when he walked in.

"Gentlemen, can I speak with you for a moment, please?" Jackson said, his gaze on each of them.

"One second, the nurse is giving us an update," Craig said.

"No, I'm not. I asked you to go to the waiting room like everyone else and someone will contact you when we know something about your erm ... brother." Her brow lifted as she said the last word.

Considering all three of them were different ethnicities, Jackson understood the doubt in her voice. They turned and headed toward the waiting room. The tall one, Derrick, looked over his shoulder at the nurse, opened his mouth, and then closed it. He filed into the room behind the other two.

Jackson suspected these three were on emotional overload. Now wouldn't be the best time to question them, but he wanted to get any information while it was fresh. He held out his hand.

"I'm Jackson. Leo and I work cases together and will do more in the future."

Craig shook his hand. "I saw you this morning at the office."

"Yeah, we had an early meeting." Jackson looked at Derrick and Tag. Neither spoke nor shook his hand. "Can anyone tell me what happened? When I last talked with Leo, he said he was meeting his friends for drinks, he felt bad he'd turned down offers before." He pointed at them. "That was with you three?"

Derrick nodded. "Yeah. I saw him pull up and went out to get him. He'd just stepped away from the car ... and he fell. I still can't believe it."

"Did you see anyone who looked out of place? Someone who normally wouldn't be in that area? Someone hanging around, looking around?"

Derrick stared at his hands, closed his eyes for a few moments. "Weren't that many people to see outside the window, let me think. Two women walked by talking, laughing. A dude in jeans, a jacket walked by, he looked at the window but kept moving. When I went outside I didn't look around, I was talking to Leo." His voice softened at the end.

Jackson backed off. "Okay. Thanks, that's good."

No one spoke for the next thirty minutes while the television played in the background. Jackson left and headed to the nurse station. She held up a finger at his approach, looked at her chart, and told him Leo's room number.

Chapter 27

Leo woke slowly. An elephant sat on his eyelids, making them hard to open. His throat was dry. Dim overhead lights cast shadows in corners as he tried to make out the door to the bathroom, except it wasn't on the left side of the room.

What? Frowning, he opened his eyes wider and lifted slightly.

Confused moments passed before he remembered. He received a sole source contract offer from Thompson. Today? Yesterday? Leo wasn't sure.

The man had used Grit, Inc. to receive more money for his department so he could, well ... use Grit, Inc. more. The company had come under attack. He'd lost clients, staff and ... he'd been shot.

He moved his left arm a few inches.

"Ah," he moaned in discomfort and glanced at his bandaged shoulder. The moment he looked, sharp pain intensified and radiated through his body.

Son of a bitch shot him.

Bullet ripped clean through his shoulder. The doctor kept him in the hospital last night to make sure he was good. At some point today, he'd be released if there were no complications. The doctor said he'd been lucky, a little lower and things would've been significantly different.

Leo said a small prayer of thanksgiving again. This time he'd been lucky. He needed to make sure there was no next time. Last night after Tag, Craig, and Derrick left, Jackson returned bringing his laptop from the office and doubled security at Leo's home and business.

Timms struck out on the street cam. They couldn't identify who pulled the trigger or why. But based on Timms description, Leo thought Paco, the gang member who'd visited his office. Paco worked for Delgado, who worked for Fuller, who worked for the consortium. Didn't they get the memo? They won the contract, no need to pick on the small company anymore.

Jackson didn't think the consortium ordered the hit.

Leo mentioned Carter's frantic call, but that didn't make the leap to the shooting. They discussed Griff and Delgado, but neither of them could see either man pulling the trigger. Both were under the narrowed gaze of the law.

Leo looked at his cell phone and accessed his computer. There had been three attempts to access his program since he'd been shot, all from outside the office. He entered a few keystrokes to release the special virus he'd created for them and pressed send.

A nurse bustled into the room, clucking her tongue. "How are you feeling? Do you need pain medication?"

"Yes, please." Sharp thrusts and blistering heat attacked his shoulder.

She picked up a plastic handle connected to a long tube. "Just push this, it'll release the medicine." Her thumb depressed the top. Seconds later the hurt ebbed. Smiling, she placed the pump handle next to him on the bed.

He waited until she left, pressed the pump again, and checked his phone. The screen had cleared. His commands were in effect. Even though he doubted the intruders used personal computers to attack his system, the greeting he sent would render that computer useless but they wouldn't know that for a few days. By then he'd gather more information to form a better welcome. He set it aside. *And now, ladies and gentlemen, welcome to the battle of the gray hacks.* Who would out-hack who?

"I heard you were hurt."

Leo jerked in surprise, jarring his shoulder and thoughts. "Ow." He frowned but didn't take his eyes off Melinda as she moved closer to the bed. Clouded with worry her dark gaze met his.

His heart lifted as he sought moisture in his dry mouth. "Is this what it takes to get your attention?" he whispered, his gaze feasting on her natural beauty.

She sighed. "No. That's a terrible thing to say."

He waved to the chair for her to sit and then tried to grab his cup of water from the nightstand.

"I'll get that." She picked up the cup and placed the straw between his lips, leaving him no other choice but to drink.

He sucked hard a few times, raised his right hand and turned his head. "That's good, thanks."

She returned the cup and met his gaze. "The news said you were shot."

"I made the news?" He tried to grin, to erase the look of worry from her face.

"This isn't funny, Leo. Someone shot you, intentionally."

"I know, and laughing beats crying any day." He paused and searched her appearance. "How have you been? They treating you alright over there?"

She shrugged and looked past him. "What? Yeah. Just peachy." She paused as her gaze roamed over him.

"I … I'll get in more trouble for this, but with you getting shot." She shook her head, pulled the chair close to the bed, sat, and pulled out her phone. "Wagram was at my office yesterday, he was with another man named Fuller." She tilted her head and frowned. "Someone worked him over pretty bad. Anyway, they had a meeting with Graves and myself. Ten minutes into the meeting, Graves steps outside the door. The moment he does, Wagram offered me money to tell him about your system."

"My system?" That surprised him. She wasn't a techie and couldn't explain the complexities of Ghost.

"Yes." She swallowed hard and then met his gaze. "After I accepted your retainer, I discussed the case with the partners. I told them what I saw in your office and how awesome it was. They weren't really interested, not then. Since Wagram's secured their services, every time I turn around, Graves is asking me details about that one visit. I've gotten a lot of the details mixed up and he's been upset about that."

Leo smiled. Melinda's mind was sharp as a blade. She hadn't mixed up anything. "Don't get in trouble because of me. Tell them what you saw if it'll help make your life easier." He shrugged and the bandage on his shoulder reminded him that wasn't a good idea.

Her gaze locked with his and she shook her head slowly. "No. Not from me. If they find out anything, it'll come from another source." She looked at the closed door and then at her phone. "Listen." She pushed the play button on her phone and then reduced the volume on a conversation in progress.

Leo listened as Wagram asked question after question about him, his business and his software. When he changed his tone when Graves entered, Leo shook his head. "He's scum. They both are. With Graves out the office, Wagram can lie on you, even repeat confidential information Graves tells him and blame it on you."

"I thought of that last night and made copies of this tape. Initially I planned to send a copy to the partners as a warning, then I thought no. If they play along with Wagram, I'll sue them as well."

"You plan to quit?"

"Yes. At the end of this month. My assistant is retiring with a full benefit package, and if I leave before that I'm afraid they may find a way to take that from her."

"Would I be wrong if I said that's great news? Do you have something else lined up?"

She smiled and it warmed his heart. He extended his right hand and she took it. "Yes, I do. I'm sorry you didn't win the bid."

He squeezed her hand. She looked up, met his gaze. "Pride prompted me to submit that bid in the first place. I'm glad I didn't win." Not that he was ever a true contender anyway according to Thompson.

She searched his face and then smiled. "As long as you're okay with not winning, that's good."

"Better than okay. Are you done avoiding me?"

Her skin reddened. She opened her mouth and then closed it. On a huff, she shook her head. "I needed time and space to make a decision regarding my career without outside influences. Remember I was ready to leave the firm when they dropped you as a client, and it's a good thing you convinced me to stay. That's not the way to handle business. This time I was afraid I'd make an emotional choice instead of one that made logical sense. I needed to line up something else. In the end I realized they are an evil, sadistic sack of lying shitheads who thought I'd allow them to use me like yesterday's rag." She shook her head. "Not happening. I passed the bar to practice law and I will. Just not there."

"Sounds like you've given this a lot of thought," he said, appreciating the light of fire in her eyes.

"I have. It's going to take time and I'll be busy, but in the long run I'll be able to look at myself in the mirror. That's important." She lifted his hand and kissed the back of it. "I'm sorry for not answering or returning your calls. I was involved in a major life overhaul."

"Same here," he said, wondering if he could ever be completely honest with her, tell her about Venom and what happened in college. He'd never wanted to share that dark part of himself with anyone before but it might be nice to have one person in the world who knew him completely. "I always hoped we'd be able to pick up where we left off one day." He squeezed her hand.

"That sounds like a good idea." She smiled and then looked at the door as the doctor walked in.

"How are you feeling this morning, Leo?"

"Much better now, Doc." Leo looked at Melinda and winked.

Chapter 28

"Did we have anything to do with that shooting?" Smothers asked Wagram on their conference call.

"No. I'm just as surprised as you are. We agreed to back off and see how the wind blew with Grit. So I left it alone. Do you know anything about this, Gates?" Wagram asked.

"No, no. Although I'm not sorry it happened. Every time I think of that Leeks deal, my blood boils. How could anyone be so—"

"You did hear the part about him not being the one who used the program, right?" Smothers asked.

"He created it, makes him just as guilty," Gates snapped.

"No it doesn't. My company manufactures guns and heavy artillery," Wagram said. "That doesn't make me a murderer or a soldier. You need to remember the difference."

"We didn't have anything to do with the shooting, then who did?" Smothers asked.

"I don't care," Gates said, stubbornly.

"You should care," Smothers snapped. "Right now I bet our group holds the number one suspect spot on Grit's and Thompson's lists. Makes no difference what the cops say. They're going to believe we were involved."

For a few moments, no one spoke. It rubbed Wagram raw how the tables had turned once they realized Grit wasn't easy prey, but he'd be a team player this time. He'd put his accounting and IT departments on high alert with instructions to back up their information every hour during the day. The notion that Venom could attack his computers and wreak havoc made his hands shake. Physical files of critical information were created and stuck in his safe.

"Before all this happened I reached out, called, and left him a message. He hasn't returned my call," Smothers said.

"Me neither," Gates admitted.

"I met him briefly when I was in North Carolina earlier this week. Graves and I bumped into him and an attorney who works for Graves at a restaurant," Wagram said without divulging the second meeting.

"Did you set up a meeting with him? Maybe offer some type deal to bring him on board in stages?" Smothers said, obviously forgetting their last conversation where they all believed Jackson warned Grit against them.

"No." Wagram explained what happened at the restaurant, really playing up Grit's outrage over the unfair treatment he received from the law firm.

"Shit," Gates said. "No wonder he hasn't returned our calls. What was Graves thinking?"

"I don't know. They've apologized but he's not buying it," Wagram said.

"Smart," Smothers said. "I want nothing to do with Grit or his companies unless he wants to come on board or work with us. If not, leave him alone." He eyed Wagram through the monitor.

"What? Why are you looking at me? I haven't done anything that you haven't. He didn't return my calls either." His blood heated over the need to defend himself. Grit created a software program, big fucking deal. Somebody shot him, who gave a fuck? The consortium won. Grit lost. Time to move on.

"Call off Fuller. I heard he'd got his ass kicked by Jackson recently. You knew that would happen and kept Fuller in the area longer than necessary. This isn't a fucking game. Jackson will make Fuller disappear and then send others after you," Gates said in a low voice. "Don't fuck with him. He's barely civilized, a gift from the US Defense department."

"Thompson had Fuller fired," Wagram argued. "When a man messes with another man's livelihood, things are going to get heated."

"No, Fuller fucked up, jumped the gun, started spouting off on Grit's company, and proved his method of surveillance was obsolete. Worse, he undermined Thompson and lost," Smothers said. "Fuller's a loose cannon—"

"Who helped us win this last contract," Wagram snapped, feeling the weight of their condemnation.

"Don't you get it?" Smothers said, his tone condescending. "Thompson won. Thanks to Fuller's false alarm, the committee paid attention, really watched and liked what they saw. Thompson's claims were validated. He can offer Grit Inc. more now than if they'd had the contract at a pace suitable for a growing company."

Wagram's chest tightened as he realized they'd been played by a master gamesman. "So if we'd done nothing?"

Smothers shrugged. "Thompson would've found another way to receive funding for Grit. He has plans, big plans for that company, but Fuller would still have ears in procurement and the people who always looked after our interest would still be in place. Instead, they all lost their jobs and the new employees will be harder to manipulate after hearing what happened."

"Way to go, Wagram. You and your watcher cost us millions," Gates said, glaring into the monitor.

Wagram's gaze flicked from Gates to Smothers and then back to Gates. He chuckled. "So this is how you want to play this? Blame me for Thompson's win? Back up, we agreed on a course of action. Before Fuller did anything, we agreed he'd stop Grit's company. Rewriting history won't work."

"That's true, we did agree, none of us suspected Thompson or realized his bottom line," Smothers said. He met Wagram's gaze. "Let's be clear, leave Grit alone. Fuller does no more work for this group. None. "

Wagram wanted to scream. They'd forgotten Fuller was as battle-tested as Jackson with a shorter grasp on reality. He couldn't be tossed aside, not now, especially after losing his job.

"He works for me, not this group. I won't allow him to assist on anything related to the consortium."

Gates shook his head. "Be careful with Fuller. He's like a rabid dog right now. I hope he doesn't bite you."

Chapter 29

"Thanks for picking me up," Leo said to Jackson as he slid in the front seat of the Dodge Charger.

"No problem. I've got some information for you and there's something I want you to see."

Leo leaned back against the headrest. The medication kept the pain at bay, but his thoughts, slippery like soap, floated everywhere. "Okay." He swallowed to wet his throat and closed his eyes as the car moved.

Leo dozed.

The bumps from the dirt road woke Leo. Leo wondered where they were headed, but decided to enjoy the quiet and gazed at tree leaves in brilliant shades of gold, red, and orange. Nature's masterpiece eased his spirit and calmed his soul. Jackson stopped the car and opened his door. Leo looked around at what had to be an old plantation house in the midst of renovation. Huge alabaster columns extended to the second floor surrounded the large wraparound porch. Planks of plywood covered several windows on the second floor, whereas the first floor boasted new windows and a large double door. The front porch had been replaced, along with the railing. It seemed an enormous undertaking.

"So this is what you do in your spare time?" Leo asked as he stepped outside the car.

Color heightened Jackson's cheeks. He stared at the house as if he could see it in its former glory. "A little at a time. I bought it when I returned from my last tour, this place had been in my family for generations. My mom had memories of playing here as a girl. We lost it during her teens. I bought it from auction." He met Leo's interested gaze. "This is an important place to me. Other than the craftsmen restoring the place, you're the first person I've brought here. Come, I want to show you something." He pulled a bag from beneath the seat and walked toward the back.

Leo looked around the overgrown yard filled with various fragrant plants and trees. Stacks of covered lumber and other building materials dotted the ground. Jackson had turned the corner of the house before Leo followed at a slower pace. Two older buildings in sad state of disrepair graced the backyard. Jackson dug through his bag and pulled out a few handguns, looked them over carefully, and placed them on a rickety-looking wood table.

Harsh sunlight beamed down on them. A wave of dizziness rolled over Leo as he shaded his eyes, with his palm, from the glare. He reached out and placed his hand against an old tree to remain standing. Looking around he realized just how isolated this place was. Why did Jackson have a gun and why did he bring Leo here? To finish the job? No … no they were partners. But he didn't really know Jackson. Jackson knew about Venom, could Leo have miscalculated the true identity of the snake?

Leo closed his eyes and counted to ten. *Stop this. Breathe. There's a reasonable answer for being here. Take a chance. Trust.*

"Hey, you okay?" Jackson asked, his voice coming closer.

Leo opened his eyes and read the alarm in Jackson's gaze. "Just winded, that's all. What're you doing?"

Jackson exhaled. "You are one gutsy dude who can probably create something in that brain of yours that'll end the world."

Leo's eyes widened at the ridiculous comment. "What? No I can't."

Jackson rolled his eyes. "That was obviously an exaggeration." He paused, looked over his shoulder and then back. "Look, I know you just left the hospital and your left arm's almost useless right now but…" He stared at Leo. "Someone shot at you. In broad daylight and almost killed you. I plan to teach you how to handle a gun and shoot."

"No thank you," Leo said. His gaze flicked downward to the gun on Jackson's waist and then to the table beyond.

"Yes," he stressed the word and pointed at Leo. "Things have changed now. Knowing how to use a gun doesn't mean you have to use it. What it does is gives you options. Options are good." Jackson headed toward the table as if he expected Leo to follow. When he didn't, Jackson looked over his shoulder at him. "Aren't you curious?"

"No, I've never been." Guns, bullets, instruments of torture or death held zero appeal for him.

"Someone picked one of these up, pointed it at you and released the trigger. The bullet ripped through your left shoulder, rendering it useless for several weeks. I'm not saying if you'd had a gun it would've evened the odds, chances are more people would've gotten hurt, but if someone surprises you in your home or when you're working late in your office, if they've managed to disable all your security, what would you do? Write a program?"

Did he say write a program? Leo snorted at the absurdity of the question. Jackson did have a point, people were after him. Although his weapon of choice was manipulating information, it might be nice to have options. Strange how having a bullet rip through your body, ripped away years of anti-gun thinking.

"I can only use my right hand, so …" He walked toward Jackson and looked at the different guns on the table. One looked heavy. The other was small and another medium.

Jackson pointed at the heavy looking pistol. "Colt 45, this one's single action." He picked it up and gave a few more details about the weapon. "In your present condition I wouldn't let you use this. It's heavy with a strong kick."

"Thanks." Leo had no interest in anything that large.

"This is a Smith and Wesson .38 caliber. Not as heavy as the Colt." He handed it to Leo. "Hold it, see how it feels."

Leo accepted the weapon, placed his finger on the trigger, lifted it, and looked toward the trees. It wasn't too heavy. He returned it to Jackson ready to get this lesson over with.

Jackson pointed to the last gun. "This baby here is a Smith and Wesson .22 Magnum." He lifted it and caressed the metal. "This works best when you're close to your target, but it'll get the job done. I think you should practice with this." He handed it to Leo.

"Feels okay, not bad." Leo lifted the gun, pointed it at the tree line, and then handed it to Jackson.

"Look, I know guns aren't your thing, let's hope you never need to use one, but I had a man covering you yesterday and you were gunned down. Whatever I can teach you today, it could save your life."

Leo disagreed with that line of thought. Guns didn't save or take lives, people did. Guns were merely instruments of intent. Just as a computer virus crafted to destroy was harmless until utilized.

Jackson spent the next few minutes instructing him on the use and care of handguns. Jackson loaded the .22 Magnum with bullets and showed him the proper stand and form. Next he fired six shots at the shed.

Leo covered his ear at the sound.

"Forgot the gear, hold on." Jackson ran toward the front of the house and returned with earmuffs and protective eyewear. "Put these on." He handed the items to Leo and slid on a pair of muffs also. Jackson reloaded, raised his hand, and fired at the shed again.

The noise wasn't as bad this time. Leo followed Jackson to what amounted to an old-fashioned lean-to instead of a shed. Poles held up one wall and a rusted tin roof kept the dirt dry. Musty bales of hay lined the back wall. Sheets of targets were on ropes stretched from side to side in front of the hay.

"Try and hit the paper," Jackson said, holding Leo's arm in position. Leo pulled the trigger. Nothing happened.

"Remember what I told you about cocking the weapon?" Jackson asked and then demonstrated again how to fire.

"Right, right. I've got it," Leo said, eager to try again. He raised his arm, stared at the target, and fired. "Did I hit it?"

"Not yet. Your arm went wide. No worries. That's normal at first, especially since you can't use your left hand. How's that feeling by the way, did the kickback hurt?"

Manageable pain throbbed in Leo's left shoulder. The meds kept most of it at bay. He shrugged off Jackson's question, got in position, and fired. For the next hour he tried to hit the paper and succeeded five times. His shoulder burned. The pain meds he'd taken twice since they'd arrived no longer worked.

Hungry and thirsty, he and Jackson headed toward the car. "You did good for your first time. There are a lot of places in town where you can practice."

"Thanks for not laughing," Leo said in a dry tone. Jackson had laughed loud and often at Leo's expense.

"You're so welcome." They turned the corner and Jackson pushed Leo back against the house. Unrelenting pain radiated from his shoulder at the impact.

"Someone's here, the tires are flat," he whispered while pulling his gun from his holster and checking his ammunition.

Nausea rose in Leo's throat from the pain and fear ravishing his body. Hell, he just left the hospital today from being shot. They were miles in the middle of nowhere. Jackson edged forward and looked around the front.

A bullet whizzed by his head.

Jackson jerked back and leaned against the wall. Chest heaving, he looked down at Leo.

"Fuller?"

Jackson shrugged.

Sweat beaded on Leo's forehead and ran down his face like a leaky rag. Needles pricked his skin as his body burned. His eyelids became heavy. The need to sit for a few moments and keep his stomach calm overwhelmed him. Otherwise, he'd empty the contents. Leo slid down the side of the wall and leaned his head back.

"Hey, buddy, don't go out on me now. Damn, you're bleeding. Not much but still," Jackson said. "I need to find who's out there. When you get your breath, go to the back door and get inside, it's unlocked."

Leo didn't have the energy to respond.

The sound of gunfire roused him. Jackson peeked around the corner. Another bullet whizzed by.

"Shit. I need to get high so I can see."

Leo held his stomach and stood on shaky knees. He stuck the pistol in his pocket and moved slowly to the back door. The stench of mold, mildew, and sawdust teased his nostrils as he inched forward in the hot room. Sweat poured down his face before he made it into the kitchen and leaned against the wall.

Dots floated in front of his eyes as he slid down the wall onto the floor, his hand on his cell phone in his pocket.

Chapter 30

Melinda walked into Grit, Inc. and looked at Cherise. "Hi, how's it going?" she asked to get social pleasantries out the way before finding Leo.

He'd been released from the hospital but wasn't at home. She'd picked up his favorites from the French restaurant and planned a nice evening for them if she could find the man.

"I'm good." Cherise looked around Melinda. "Is the boss with you?"

"No. I thought he was here." Now she was more confused.

"One second, let me ask Barb." She placed a call. A few seconds later Barb strode out front wearing her signature black leather vest, jeans, boots, and button down shirt.

"Jackson picked him up over an hour ago. They had some things to discuss and he planned to go home to follow the doctor's orders. I've tried to call him, but it doesn't go through," Barb said frowning.

"See if you can find him on the monitor," Cherise said, walking around her desk toward the console room.

Craig sat in the room working on equipment. He looked up when they entered. "Hey, Melinda, what's going on?"

Barb repeated her concerns.

Craig looked at the monitor and the blue dots. "You do realize Leo has to unlock the system for anyone to use it, right?" His gaze swept over them. "He's big on security, and I may not be able to get in." Craig typed in his code and asked for a simple search.

The system refused.

"Does that no in red mean something?" Melinda asked, both scared that something may be wrong with Leo and fascinated by how his brain worked.

"Yeah, after three times it locks out my password and Leo has to reset everything, including giving me a new password," Craig said.

"Okay, we'll take turns," Barb said taking the seat next to him and then entered her password. "Search for specific E&E."

The system refused again. The bold red letters reminded Melinda of Leo. She could see him sitting at a computer, creating that response.

"Okay, we have two more shots, I'm not taking it to the max of three. If you have any ideas, speak," Craig said, staring at the moving dots on the monitor.

"Ask for location of Administrator," Cherise said.

"Okay, that might work," Craig said and typed it in. This time when the system refused, Craig stood with his hands in the air and moved away.

Barb remained at the console staring at the dots.

"Ask for Leo by name," Melinda said, considering the man set everything up so that he'd be involved, he shouldn't have a problem with staff knowing his location.

Barb nodded and typed in the query. The screen changed and zeroed in on a lone blue dot a good distance from everyone. The dot held Leo's initials above it.

"Where the hell is that?" Craig asked, retaking his seat and pulling out a keyboard connected to another system. He typed in the latitude and longitude numbers and received information on the land.

"Is there anyone near him?" Melinda asked, pulling out her phone. She called Bronson who she met during the Drake murder investigation. She suspected he was interested in her on a personal level when he gave her his personal number.

"Near, no," Craig said. "Even if they were, we can't activate anyone." He stood, pulled out his phone, and headed toward the door. "But it's only twenty minutes from town. I can drive out there. Hello, Derrick?" Craig left.

Bronson answered. "Hello, Melinda, this is a pleasant surprise."

"I know, but it's an emergency." She explained everything and when he heard Jackson had picked Leo up, he had her repeat the location and promised to get on it.

Melinda and Barb shared a look. "I don't want to just wait here," Barb said.

"Me neither," Melinda said.

"Nope, I can't leave, neither can you ladies. We have a new client coming in thirty minutes. You'll need to rope him in Barb, get that signature on the bottom line," Cherise said.

"Thirty minutes? Leo hadn't planned to come in today, why is there a sales appointment?"

"Only day he's in town, I guess. I'm not handling it, that's for sure," Cherise said as she returned to her office.

Barb looked close to tears.

Melinda didn't have the heart to leave her behind. "I'll stay here. Bronson promised to send an update as soon as he found something."

Barb nodded and then looked at her. "Aren't you supposed to be at work?"

"No, I took off to celebrate another attorney taking the good doctor as their client and Leo's release from the hospital," Melinda said, following Barb back to the training room.

Chapter 31

Leo's body burned from the inside. His breath came in short gasps. Turning to the side, he emptied his stomach and then gagged at the stench. His chest expanded as he filled his lungs with air.

Wincing at the pain in his shoulder, he climbed into a kneeling position and tried to crawl. His shoulder said no. He struggled to stand. Several excruciating moments later, he leaned against the wall and looked around.

Organized chaos.

Subfloors had been redone and the plastered walls were in the process of being replaced with sheetrock. Stacks of materials were everywhere, giving the floor a patch-quilt appearance.

Leo moved.

Gunfire erupted outside, reminding him of the risky situation. He patted the pistol in his pocket and prayed never to use it. Moving slowly in the opposite direction from the shots, he pulled out his phone and cursed. No signal. He couldn't call, but he'd show up on the monitor, that's if they realized he was missing, which wasn't likely since he hadn't been gone that long. *Damn.* Situations like this made a good argument for him sharing access to Ghost when he wasn't available. Definitely something to think about.

God he was thirsty. He looked around for something, anything to ease his parched throat and found nothing. His stomach, now empty, rumbled. He touched his shoulder. It was damp from before, but the bleeding had stopped, thank goodness. In fact, he felt a lot better after clearing his stomach. Leaving the kitchen, he stepped into a wide open area. The wooden stairs had been replaced but not stained. Leo headed up rather than go outside.

Maybe he'd be able to see who flattened the tires or find Jackson. It'd been quiet since he heard the last gunfire. One thing for sure, they weren't talking over their differences. When he reached the landing, all six doorways lacked doors. The pervading darkness reminded him of the boarded windows he'd noticed when they arrived, with the exception of one. Light flowed onto the hardened wood floors that protested each step he took toward that beacon at the back of the house. He wondered why Jackson hadn't covered that window. When he reached the opening, he peeked in, his hand resting on his cell phone out of habit.

A bed sat in the middle of the room near the open window. Air moved through the screened windows. An old wooden chair and beat-up desk sat in the corner. The room appeared feminine and Leo wondered if this had been Jackson's mother's room as a child.

More gunfire erupted.

Leo dropped to his knees, jarring his shoulder. A moment later he scooted to the high window and peeked outside. Strong, towering trees and years of overgrowth blocked his view. He strained his eyes to see Jackson. A movement in the tree near the house drew his gaze. Squinting, he tried to see if a squirrel or a similar animal played in the tree, which made no sense with random gunfire. Remaining still, he continued to stare at the tree. Something moved again.

Jackson ran toward the back porch. The close sound of gunfire hurt.

"Yes," the male voice said, the sound of satisfaction penetrated the ringing in Leo's ears.

Sure the person outside the window in the tree wasn't Jackson, Leo pulled the gun from his pocket, removed the safety, pointed toward the tree and fired.

The scream echoed in Leo's mind as the man fell. Leo looked out the window to see someone moaning and moving slowly on top of a stack of wood.

"Ouch, that hurt," he murmured and leaned forward for a better view.

Two men lay below. One was Jackson. He had no idea who the other was.

Leo turned to go assist Jackson when he saw several cases of water in the closet along with jerky and other foodstuffs. "Thank you, thank you." He pounced on the bottled water, drinking two in succession. He stuffed several bottles and snacks in a pillow case and headed downstairs.

As Leo stepped out the back door, he saw Sam Fuller crawling to Jackson. Leo dropped the pillowcase, picked up a light board, and swung, knocking Fuller across his back. He couldn't imagine the kind of training that'd enable a person to ignore his body to continue his quest.

"Argh." Leo dropped his makeshift weapon and grabbed his arm. "Leave him alone, asshole. This is over. You're bleeding, he's bleeding, hell, I'm bleeding. This can be continued when we're healthy again if you want."

"No, we'll finish this right now," Fuller grunted, blood streaming down his face. "I want him dead for what he did."

Leo moved closer to Jackson and retrieved Jackson's gun. Tired of the bullshit, he pointed it at Fuller.

Fuller laughed. "You can't shoot worth a damn." He coughed, spit out reddish fluid and glanced at Leo. "I only fell because you shot me in the foot, Only an idiot shoots a man in his foot." He spit more blood from his mouth toward Leo's feet. "Just one of us will leave here alive today, and you should know I don't have much to live for anymore."

"Did you pay someone to shoot me yesterday? Did Wagram tell you to do it? The consortium?" Leo wanted answers.

Fuller spit again. "Damn right I did, should'a done it myself. Half blind punk shoots almost as bad as you. Sissies said to back off, leave you alone. Unacceptable. Son of a bitch missed should've got you."

"Why?" Leo couldn't understand why Fuller would try to kill him if he hadn't been ordered to do it.

"You don't win." He pointed at Leo. "You can't win. Don't give a fuck about that shit you created, don't make you a winner ... not in my book. Still a boy hiding in the shadows like a punk. Some kid is spending time in prison for what you made. How's that make you feel?"

Leo tensed and glanced at Jackson. He tried to never think of the kid who stole his program and took a couple steps back.

"Think we don't know it was you who made that shit that hit the trading company way back, they know, scared them."

Leo couldn't speak past the ball of fear lodged in his throat. The consortium suspected he'd created Venom? Why hadn't they threatened to expose him? Were they waiting for a better time? What should he do?

"You don't know what you're talking about," Leo said hedging for time.

Fuller snorted and then coughed. "Fuck you. You're a fucking criminal, I hope they grow balls and turn you in."

So they didn't plan to turn him in, start an investigation? Great news, but why? Not that he wasn't happy to hear he didn't need to relocate to a third world country but it was hard to accept this bit of news without wondering.

Determined he would take his involvement with Venom to the grave, Leo shrugged. "You've got the wrong guy, besides they won the contract, why'd you attack me?"

Fuller snorted. "They won, but I lost everything to make that happen, and you're still standing. Jackson's still standing and covering for you, said the same thing that you didn't create the virus, it's all a lie. Unacceptable." He tried to remove the knife strapped to his leg and couldn't.

Leo saw the deadness in Fuller's eyes. The man really believed what he said. No one should be so void of hope and full of hatred. What could make a man this way? Even with the threat of prison hanging over his head, he'd tried to make it right in his own way by helping people. Never once did he imagine not living or merely existing like Fuller. He thought back to Fuller's bio. "What about Amelia?"

Fuller jerked and then narrowed his eyes. "I'll kill you for mentioning her name." He reached for his gun but the holster was empty.

"Why not live for her? Spend time getting to know your daughter. She's in college. Smart, kind, and loving. What's wrong with living for her?" Leo continued down this path not because he thought Fuller would share but because he needed to be sure he never became this void of life.

Fuller's face reddened and he screamed. The anguish in his voice caused the hairs on Leo's arms to rise. Pain, mixed with despair, lodged on Fuller's face as his shoulders slumped and his gaze slid over Jackson, the house, and then back to Leo.

"Shut the hell up. You don't know anything," Fuller growled, his eyes glassy.

Leo pushed. Anyone who knew him would say Leo Grit didn't pry into other people's lives. Usually he didn't care. But Jackson was injured. Leo had no idea what was wrong with him. He couldn't turn his back on Fuller to help Jackson, so he dealt with Fuller first. Leo couldn't shoot the man, not unless his life was threatened and he didn't feel defenseless. More like pity, sadness, and hurt for this man who'd served his country with pride to be reduced to his current state.

"Does Amelia know you at all? What if she longs to talk to her father one last time?"

"She doesn't," Fuller snapped.

"If she doesn't know you, whose fault is that?"

Fuller pointed at him. "I had to leave on a two-year assignment. She was three." He closed his eyes. "My little princess," he whispered. "But two years was too long to wait. Her mom met someone else. Someone who never put his life on the line, someone who took care of my princess while I helped to make their world safe. When I came back, I sued for visitation, but they kept moving. By the time I tracked them down, Amelia had two younger sisters and she called this man 'Daddy.' She had no time for me or memories of me. When she asked me to leave her alone, I did as she asked."

Damn. That snapshot of family life left Leo speechless. He couldn't think of anything else to say.

Fuller chuckled. "You should see your face."

Heat flooded Leo's cheeks. "Who does shit like that?"

Fuller grunted and rolled onto his back. A long gash across his stomach bled steadily. "You'd be surprised. Working for Uncle Sam can cost more than an arm or leg. It'll cost you your heart. How's a man supposed to live without his heart?" Fuller asked the question so softly if Leo hadn't been listening hard, he'd have missed it.

Unable to think of an intelligent answer, Leo stared at Fuller who placed his arm across his forehead and his other hand above his wound. Blood dripped from the hole in Fuller's shoe. Why wasn't the man screaming from the pain?

"You're bleeding," Leo said, feeling useless as he stated the obvious. "Do you have a first aid kit in your car?"

"It's a rental, asshole."

Leo glared at him and then stepped back to look at Jackson. He couldn't see where the bullet hit. There wasn't that much blood on the ground, not like Fuller's anyway.

"Why can't I get a damn signal to call the paramedics?" Leo said.

"Not for me," Fuller said his voice raspy. "I'm done. As long as my daughter is taken care of that's all I care about. She may not have wanted anything to do with me, but I've got her and my grandchildren covered. I want her to have it." He looked at Leo for a few moments and then licked his lips. "She was the cutest thing, running around the house, dark curls flying, asking me to chase her." He chuckled. "She loved chocolate. Always wanted it on her food. Chocolate in milk ... yes, but on French fries?" Fuller chuckled and then coughed up blood.

"Be still, you landed on that stack of wood. Take it easy," Leo said, looking around for a way to help. He heard something, the roar of an engine in the distance.

Several engines.

His heart raced as he stared toward the front of the house. *Please, please let someone get here before dark to help these men.* Leo would try to drag them inside, but with one arm he wasn't sure he could.

A car door slammed. And then another. "Leo?" Craig yelled.

Heat radiated through his chest as recognition slammed into him. They'd come, somehow his team found him. "Back here," Leo said. "We're back here." Tears of gratitude filled his eyes as Craig, Derrick, Bronson and another man ran toward them. The sweet sound of the paramedic's siren buoyed his spirits. He wiped his eyes and moved out the way as Bronson and the other man examined Jackson and then Fuller.

"This one needs help first," Bronson told the paramedics as they rushed to the back and attended Fuller who'd gone silent.

Craig and Derrick helped him to move out of the way. They sat on the back porch and watched the paramedics work on Fuller. Leo explained the fall from the tree onto the boards. Another ambulance arrived for Jackson, and Leo insisted on riding with him. Bronson finally agreed and promised to lock up the house as well as securing Jackson's gear.

During the ride to the hospital, Leo covered Jackson's hand. "You're going to be alright, partner. Hang in there buddy."

If Jackson hadn't worried over Leo's inability to protect himself none of this would've happened and that would've been a shame. In the past few hours Leo came face to face with the shame of his past and realized there were worst things. No, he'd never admit to creating Venom, but he wouldn't half-live either. He and Jackson were partners, tomorrow was a new day and he wanted to see it.

Chapter 32

Three days later, Leo and Melinda entered his office. She'd been his constant companion since he returned from the hospital with Jackson. He liked it.

Barb, Cherise, and Craig met him in the reception area with cheers and smiles. Leo still laughed when he thought of how Cherise kept Barb and Melinda from being underfoot by telling them a client would be coming in. By the time she told them the third time that the client called saying he was running late, they realized her game.

Leo kissed Cherise on the cheek in gratitude. The last place he would've wanted Melinda or Barb was around an unstable Fuller.

Fuller had been granted his wish and died on the operating table from internal bleeding. Leo had been tempted to write his daughter a scathing letter regarding her cruelty to a man who served his country before he turned into a murdering asshole.

Melinda advised him against it, and from a legal standpoint he realized she was right. They'd just flown in from Fuller's memorial service in Virginia.

Barb hugged him. "Glad to see you back."

"Glad to be seen," Leo said, grinning at her.

Craig offered his fist bump and a huge smile. "You look much better than the last time I saw you."

Leo squeezed Melinda's waist. "Feel better too. It's good to be back." He looked around the office and then at Barb. "What do we have going on?"

"Training new decoys, and we've had three new job requests over the past two days. Oh yeah, Jackson's office called. He wants you to call him when you get in."

"Will do." He turned and kissed the back of Melinda's hand. "Time to get to work. If you're serious about renting office space downstairs, contact the leasing agent, let me know what they say."

"Yeah ... no. That's too close. I've told you I'm accepting a position with another firm downtown. Stop trying to manipulate me." She pulled her hand from his and blew him a kiss. "I've got work to do."

Leo smiled and headed to his office.

Jackson hadn't been seriously injured. The bullet hit him in the head, but didn't penetrate his skull. He fell on a rock which caused him to blackout. He hadn't been happy when Leo placed everything on hold to attend Fuller's memorial, but after Leo repeated what amounted to Fuller's last conversation, Jackson didn't say anything else.

He closed his door, ran a scan on all systems and called Jackson. So far they hadn't heard anything from the consortium about venom or anything else. Jackson said one of them reached out to Thompson and he warned them away. Leo hadn't done anything with the information he'd collected on the three men and wouldn't. Fair competition was fine, and as long as they left him and his alone, he'd do the same.

"Ready to get some work done?" Jackson said when he came on the phone.

"Yeah, what's up?" Leo's left shoulder was still stiff, but he could tap the keys on the board.

"Thompson sent two jobs. Both in Raleigh. We need as many E&Es as we can find."

Leo smiled. "Good, that's my specialty."

<<<<>>>>

Hello,

Thank you for taking the time to read Decoy U, Eyes & Ears Everywhere, case of the Conniving Contractors. I love a story with good dramatic tension that's not too over the top, with an interesting twist. Writing stories about people who could live next door, with ordinary struggles that change without warning feeds my creative energies.

Decoy U – Eyes & Ears Everywhere series follow the cases of Leo Grit and Jackson, his new partner, as they face interesting jobs to assist Barnaby Thomas and Detective Bronson prevent criminal activities and solve crimes. An unlikely pair, Leo and Jackson each bring necessary qualities to the table to get the job done while dealing with their personal challenges and those of their staff.

You're invited to journey with me through all the books in this new series. If you like fast paced action, suspense and interesting connections like me, you won't be disappointed. Feel free to drop me a line, Anita@AnitaMooring.com or like my FaceBook page: Decoy U. Also you can find me at my website, www.Anita Mooring.com.

Take a moment and sign up for my Newsletter to receive information on new releases, works in progress and to win cool Decoy U items you can't get anywhere else. As a special bonus for signing up, you'll receive a special gift. The *Decoy U Companion* book with pictures and bios of the employees at Grit, Inc. Click this sign up link and get your copy today! Thank you. (http://anitamooring.com/**newsltr-sign-up**/)

If you enjoyed reading Decoy U, the case of the Conniving Contractors, I'd like to ask a favor. When you finish reading, please leave a review, whatever your opinion, I assure you I appreciate it.

Thanks again
Anita